A LOVE NOVEL BY
C.B. ATKINS

NEVER TOO LATE TO Bloom

Contents

Acknowledgements

I must give a special thanks to my fabulous husband who inspires me to go beyond my comfort zone and pursue dreams bigger than I ever imagined. My wonderful children and grandchildren are the light of my life, whom I am eternally grateful for. I must thank Dr. Joseph L. Ross, a man who saw in me what I did not see in myself. He is my mentor and spiritual advisor. Lastly, I must recognize a hero, New York's Governor Andrew Cuomo, who addressed the American people daily during the COVID-19 pandemic. One night he spoke words that birthed life into me while I quarantined myself for 14 days. I must paraphrase his words, but he indicated that he knew it was a trying time for everyone and he encouraged Americans to use this time to reunite with family, write, paint and make the time valuable. It was on that night that I was inspired to write a book that was housed in me for years but that I was just too busy to write. Thank you to everyone who has ever believed in me, inspired me, and encouraged me.

The Seed Stage

*M*any people have never heard of Black Mountain, North Carolina. It is a small town that attracts seasonal tourism and a place that is home to many Christian retreats. Black Mountain was named for the old train stop at the Black Mountain Depot, which is located at the end of the Black Mountain range of the Blue Ridge Mountains in the Southern Appalachians. Black Mountain, North Carolina has always been a great place to live. The main streets are packed with shops and galleries filled with the handiwork of local and regional artists. You can always find an establishment that has live music on stage almost every night of the week. There are a variety of stage plays that include both local and national acts. Accommodations are never an issue and are readily available to all tourists and guests. You never have to worry about a place to stay.

The population is small, and the behavior displayed in a small town is a lot different than that of a large city. Everyone is family oriented and looks out for each other. Some people call it Southern hospitality, but I like to think of it as just displaying pure human compassion. My grandparents, Adam French and Lillian French, never discussed with me how things were when they moved to Black Mountain in the 1960s, however, my parents, Adam French, II and Bethany French, always rave about their upbringing in a small town. I liked my small town and yet, I could not wait to go away to college to experience the big city life. My plan was to attend Stanford

University in Stanford, California for my undergrad and Yale University in New Haven, Connecticut for law school.

I was born in March. I am told that March 8, 1982 was a mild day with temperatures that reached about 72 degrees. My mother's water broke, and my grandmother called the midwife. I was born in one of the six beautiful rooms of my grandparents' home. I am the first of seven children and never could understand how my father and mother juggled their careers as a lawyer and a psychologist to have so much quality time that our family expanded from two to nine people. My mother and father are very hard workers. We were not rich, but we certainty had a magnificent upbringing. My siblings and I are all one to two years apart. My parents told me their plans were to have ten children, because they both were the only children to their parents, although my maternal grandmother adopted three girls, which gave me the privilege of having my Aunt Beatrice, Aunt Maretta, and Aunt Autumn, who I was named after. I do not remember a lot about my childhood and my family did not come into full focus until I reached the age of 12. Anything before my twelfth year on earth is foggy, but reality sharpened for me during my teen years. All I know is that I had a wonderful family that was rich in love and who worked hard so we could have some of the finer things in this life.

My grandparents pushed the importance of education into my dad and he passed that same value on to his children. As for my grandfather's education, he learned his business savvy from the prominent residents of Black Mountain, North Carolina. With years of making the right investments and submitting his life to God, my grandfather made a good life for my father and instilled many good values in him. Spreading God's Love Ministries International has a membership of over 2,000 people and my grandfather is the pastor. Of course, my grandmother is the first lady and is satisfied with just looking fabulous and sitting in the back of the church. My grandfather's life mission was to groom my father to take over the ministry, but my father never received that spiritual call from God, so he serves as a deacon and became my grandfather's right-hand man. Every time my father would tell the story he would look at my mother and both would laugh. My father often joked about the mounts of pressure he was under, being the only child. My father had a twin brother, but his brother was stillborn at birth and my dad always joked about how he was gifted with both of their strength. I speculate that the process of training was not easy, but my father landed on top with a beautiful wife, well-mannered children, a successful career, and a comfortable life.

Now I cannot leave out my Uncle Malcom, who has been my father's best friend since they were children. They both went to college together, although they chose different career paths. My dad chose the law profession and my Uncle Malcom chose the teaching profession. After many years of hard work, Uncle Malcolm was chosen to become the superintendent of all public schools in Black Mountain. My Uncle Malcolm has dated many women, but he always likes to say he never found the right one for him to marry. He gets a new Land Rover every two years, so I imagine that is his favorite vehicle. I made the mistake of once asking Uncle Malcom what type of woman he was looking for. He gave me such a long list, I knew he would always be single, and it made sense why he dated so many. No one woman could ever contain everything he had on that list, unless she was cloned from several different women. Uncle Malcom always ended each question concerning marriage with, "I have not been as lucky as Adam in finding the right woman to love." I would have to agree. I have heard my parents argue and disagree in private, but in front of the outside world they always appear as the perfect couple. After being together for 42 years and married for 39, I would have to agree, they are not the perfect couple, but they are the ideal couple.

I came into this world as an offspring of the French clan and the beginning of the third generation. There were high expectations already set for me. I was given the obligation to keep family traditions and a level of pressure to form a personal relationship with God. I was the only daughter of Adam and Bethany French and the eldest child. I had six younger brothers. Our upbringing was not of a privileged childhood. The most memorable times of our childhood are from Thanksgiving , Christmas, and the entire week of the Easter holiday. We were raised knowing that it is better to give than to receive. We did not have extravagant clothes or toys, yet we were always given the best with the intention that it is what we needed and not wanted. For example, I was given an Apple laptop because I needed it for my schoolwork, then I was given an Apple desktop. Designer clothes were not my parents' specialty, but shopping at upscale stores was their choice. My mom would say, "When you buy good quality stuff you have it for a long time." I must admit she is correct. Many of my clothes are still being passed around to different people.

We did not have eloquent dinners, but we had family dinners. My parents are big about family gathering around the table together. During the Thanksgiving and Christmas holidays my parents would not just have family over, but neighbors as well. The menu would always be Southern cuisine: fried chicken, collard greens, macaroni and cheese, sweet potatoes, turkey, stuffing, and cranberry sauce). There would be an abundance of deserts: cakes, pies, banana pudding, etc. My parents spoiled us with love, attention, and great values. It was during my childhood that I recognized that the seeds were planted for me to bloom.

Hey Bud (Germination)

CHAPTER 2

*F*rom the time I was born, I was always read to, taught the alphabet, taught how to count, taught the Bible, and taught how to pray. When I reached the age of ten, I was very active in the church and was promoted from third to sixth grade in school. I adopted my love for education from my parents, who were avid learners.

The Charles D. Owen High School was notorious for having big events for seniors to lead up to graduation day. All my friends were getting ready for the spring dance and hoping that certain boys would ask them to the dance. That was not my concern and I was convinced that I was not going to attend. I wanted to focus on graduating and getting into college, so I made a vow that I would not date or go out with any boys until I graduated college. Some of my school mates asked me to go out or to date, but I refused and, quite frankly, my parents would not have approved anyway. My friend's brother, Paul Butler, was one of the best-looking guys in town, and he asked me to the dance. I used the excuse that I could not date. After all, he was older than me. It was believable because just about everyone in town knew of my parents and grandparents' religious stance. Most of them attended my grandfather's church or knew someone who did. I politely turned down Paul and when my parents asked if I was going to the dance, I pleaded with them to not make me go. I would not be surprised if they had a date arranged for me with someone's son or grandson in the church.

I graduated from high school at the age of 16. I had to keep my focus and follow my plan, so I went directly to college, but because of my age, my parents would not allow me to leave the state of North Carolina. They did allow me to live on campus, though. That may not seem like much to some, but this was a big deal for me. After all, they were allowing their only daughter to move away from home. My parents would call at least ten times a day with the same questions: "Did you eat? Is anyone bothering you? Are you taking time to pray?" The answers to the questions were always, "Yes, Mom. No, Mom. Yes, of course, Mom," when in fact, I knew I was not making time to pray. The fact is, I was only focused on my goal of graduating and becoming a successful lawyer. I refused to even date for fear it would derail my dreams.

The transition from high school to college was not easy, but I was determined and set an expanded goal to become an attorney by the age of 23. While other students were enjoying summer break, going on wonderful trips, I was taking summer classes. I had become so wrapped up in school it left little time for church. My grandfather and father often reminded me that God was the foundation of my life and the secret to my success.

Toward the end of my sophomore year, my roommate, April, insisted that I go to the birthday party of her friend, Destiny, who she had known for years. I did not know Destiny and could not even recall meeting her. I was 18 years old now, and although I was still shy and reserved, I felt comfortable going with April. She had been my roommate for over two years, and I trusted her. I knew she would not put me in any danger. I got Destiny a birthday card and put $25 inside of it, because I was taught not to go to a party empty handed. Destiny and I connected right away, and she was so nice. I learned she was a resident of Gastonia, North Carolina and, like me, she was a sophomore. After April and Destiny walked away, I proceeded to find a corner. I had never been to this type of party before, where people danced, drank alcoholic beverages, and gathered in small groups with people who were not their family or close friends. I felt someone staring at me, so I began to scope out the room. Then I noticed the most handsome guy I had ever seen looking directly at me. The ironic thing was that I could not keep my eyes off him either. He was tall, nicely built, fair-complexioned, and well-groomed. I began to wonder if I caught his attention because of my obvious discomfort level and the fact that I was pushed up in a corner, while everyone else was laughing, talking, and mingling. In my mind I was thinking, *this is the man of my dreams*. I became nervous and my heart was pounding. After all, I had lived a pretty sheltered life and here I was, 18 years old and having never dated or kissed anyone in my life outside of my family's cheek kisses. I had many suitors, but I had a life goal and I could not risk being derailed by my heart or my emotions. The focused mindset I had provided people who did not know me with labels to attach to me—labels such as *stuck up*, *bougie*, *too good*, and *high and mighty*." Theses labels were hurtful, because that was not who I was at all. I was a girl who had plans and life was causing me to bud into the woman I dreamed of being my whole life.

The next thing I knew this handsome man was walking toward me. His first words were, "Are you okay?"

"Yes, I am okay," I replied.

He then extended his hand and said, "I am Matthew Buddy Dorsey, III. My friends call me Buddy."

"Hi. I am Autumn French."

We both attended Duke University. He majored in biology and I majored in criminal justice. I learned that we both were pressured by our roommates to attend this party. Buddy said, "It is obvious you do not want to be here." We both laughed. He was right, I did not want to be where I was, and I had a lot of homework to complete. Buddy asked me if I wanted him to walk me back to my dorm. I was hesitant. I did not know him and I did not know if April knew him. Then I noticed April heading in my direction.

"Hey Autumn, why are you not mingling?" asked April. Buddy stood there waiting on my response. "Hi, Buddy," my roommate said. That was my cue that she knew this handsome man who had sparked something within me.

"April, Buddy is going to walk me back to our dorm," I said, waiting for her response.

"Make sure she gets there safely, Buddy," she replied. That eased my suspicion and I felt comfortable with Buddy walking me back to the dorm. Buddy and I laughed all the way back to the dorm.

"You are beautiful inside and out," he said. Of course. I blushed. Several guys had told me I was beautiful, but no one had ever referred to my inner self or character. Buddy asked for my telephone number and of course I gave it to him. I did not want to appear desperate, so I did not ask for his number, and from my upbringing, I felt it was appropriate for him to make the first move. I did not want my shyness and inexperience with the opposite sex to show. I had six brothers who were not far from me in age, so I did have some form of experience with the male species, but not in this capacity. That night I labeled Matthew Buddy Dorsey, III the man I wanted to spend the rest of my life with.

When April got in, I had a slew of questions about Buddy. April, Destiny, and Buddy were all from the same town, Gastonia,

North Carolina. So, I cut right to it, "April, does Buddy have a lot of girlfriends?"

April said, "I only remember Buddy dating one person and she dropped him for someone else. Buddy is a good guy with a great family." I was relieved and knew that I could now let some of my guard down.

The very next morning, Buddy called me and asked if he could take me to lunch. It was Saturday and I did not have any classes, so I was free. I was so excited to hear from him and was quite surprised he called so quickly. Then I stopped and looked in the mirror and said, "Autumn, you cannot lose your focus and be derailed from your dreams." It was settled in my heart that no matter what transpired between Buddy and I, I would remain focused on my goal of being an attorney by the age of 23. Buddy and I talked for hours. The more we talked the more we realized how much we had in common. We both came from small towns and were brought up with strict religious backgrounds. Gastonia was 93 miles from Black Mountain. I was only an hour and a half drive away from Buddy's hometown. Buddy had already obtained his license and his parents had him a car. Buddy was soon to be three years older than me. At the end of the evening Buddy tried to kiss me but I refused to get caught up in any emotional relationship, so I quickly turned my face, so his lips met my cheek.

We spent a lot of time together during the entire school year. The more time we spent together the more I became comfortable with him and was convinced that he was the man for me. Buddy would often tell me, "I am going to marry you one day." After six months we took our relationship to the next level. We would stay in each other's dorms when our roommates had plans to stay out. I confided in Buddy that I had never be in a sexual relationship with any man, which made me a virgin. Buddy was so understanding and supportive of my life choice to wait and proceed with caution in going all the way with any man. We would sleep with our clothes on, kiss, and just hold each other closely. This was a regular thing for about a year.

On my nineteenth birthday I went home to Black Mountain and Buddy went home to Gastonia. Buddy and I talked on the telephone at least ten times a day during the entire weekend we were apart. In addition to my birthday, my family and I were rejoicing because I was about to graduate from Duke and had gotten accepted to Yale University. Yes, that's right, I was going to law school. I could see my dreams unfolding before eyes.

When I returned to campus, Buddy and I held each other like we had not seen each other in years. Buddy asked if we could get a hotel room because he had a very special gift for me and he wanted to have a private dinner with me. I felt so special because Buddy was going all out for me. Buddy requested that I wear something nice because it would be a formal dinner for just the two of us. "I will pick you up at 5:00 PM," said Buddy.

"I will be ready," I replied. I found the most eloquent dress and heels I owned. In fact, they were new. We arrived at the hotel; Buddy had reserved a beautiful suite. The room was filled with flowers and our dinner was there awaiting us in silver trays. Neither of us drank, so Buddy ordered a non-alcoholic champagne. I ran to the window to look at the beautiful view. I heard the cork pop and I began to get nervous again. I had butterflies in my stomach. I began to feel nervous and question if I made the right decision by coming to this hotel alone with Buddy. Before I ran out the room, I turned quickly to see what Buddy was doing. Buddy was down on one knee, holding a beautiful diamond ring in his hand. He said, "Autumn. please do me the great honor of being my wife soon. Will you please marry me?"

Before I knew it, I said, "Yes!" It was as if the word just rolled out of my mouth without any thought or usage of the brain. We sealed the proposal with a kiss. This kiss was different than any other kiss that Buddy and I had ever shared. The next thing I knew we were laying on the bed, but this time instead of holding each other passionately, Buddy was slowly undressing me. My mind was yelling *stop*, but my mouth never uttered a word. I guess this was what people meant when they talked about hormones running rampant. I had committed my all to Buddy. He had to be my first and I was determined he would be my one and only. Guilt began to rise, but then I quickly justified my actions by telling myself we are engaged, and we are going to spend our lives together. I was in a lot of pain. It hurt so badly, but Buddy had a right to be with me and this was the way to show him I was his forever. At least that is what I told myself. When he finished, blood was all over the bed. Buddy said, "You were a virgin."

I looked at Buddy while in pain, shocked because it appeared that he did not believe me. Yet I said, "Yes." That night changed the dynamics of our entire relationship. We began to be more intimate and never thought about birth control. We met each other's families and shared our marriage plans with them. Everyone agreed we would not get married until I graduated from law school and Buddy graduated from medical school. During the summer I would stay with Buddy and his family, and Buddy would also stay with me and my family. All of us had built a bond. I had learned so much about Buddy's family and Buddy had learned so much about mine. Buddy was expected to take over his family practice and I was expected to be a partner within my dad's law firm. The most important thing was that we had received our families' blessings.

Buddy and I both graduated in May and that August he was entering medical school at John Hopkins University in Baltimore, Maryland and I was off to Yale University in New Haven, Connecticut. Buddy and I had our lives mapped out. Each holiday we would meet in North Carolina and equally share our time with our families, as well as with each other. Buddy and I promised to graduate with honors and then begin our lives together as husband and wife.

We got settled into graduate school and in the beginning, we would speak every day. Our class demands caused our calls to lessen, but each time we did speak, we would declare our love for one another. During the second year of graduate school, I went back to North Carolina for Thanksgiving and the winter break, but Buddy could not. For some reason, he was behind in his studies and he had to make up his assignments. Of course, I was disappointed but understanding. We had made a pact and we both promised to fulfill the promise we made to each other. I kept calling Buddy, but I could not get him on phone. I began to worry because I did not want Buddy to fail and if Buddy was this busy, he must have been in serious academic trouble. When I would get Buddy on the phone it would be brief conversations because of his desire to complete all his assignments in a timely manner. I couldn't allow myself to get emotional over this. I had to stay focused. I had one more year of law school before I graduated.

I felt terribly ill during the winter break. My parents were very concerned about my well-being. I could not keep any food down, I had literally no energy, and all I could do was sleep. I knew I could not be pregnant because I continued to get my menstrual, although it began to occur in an unusual cycle. My parents took me to my family doctor. He ran every test on me imaginable. Three days later I returned to the doctor's office to get my results back. I was pregnant. The diagnosis was devastating. I sat in the doctor's examination room in unbelief. "I can't be," I said, despite all those passionate nights with Buddy and not using any protection. This was new for me. I should have confided in my mother. She would have told me to get some protection or perhaps April or Destiny would have educated me. Yet here I was, pregnant and alone.

"Should I call your mother in the room?" the doctor asked.

"Yes," I replied. "Yes." Yes was a word I needed to reevaluate, because I was in this situation because of replying yes. I asked my doctor to tell my mom. My mom stood there shocked and I saw her eyes watering.

"When are you going to tell Buddy?" she asked. I told her I would call him tonight. My doctor scheduled me an appointment with one of the best gynecologists in North Carolina. The gynecologist would do an ultrasound and a thorough exam to make sure the baby was healthy and to inform me of how far along I was.

When we got home my dad insisted we call Buddy and his parents right away. I pleaded with my dad to please let me handle it. I promised him I would. Then my dad asked what my plans about school were. I asked my dad if we could discuss that after I went to the gynecologist. The first thing my grandfather said was, "I knew something like this was going to happen when you did not make time for God in your busy schedule."

Then my dad chimed in, saying, "God is the foundation of your being and your success." Where they right? Did all this occur because I was too focused on me and my goals, while ignoring God? I did not know, but I knew my life was going to change now. When I was finally alone, I cried, I prayed, and I reasoned with myself before I came to my final decision. I would not tell Buddy about the pregnancy right now because I did not want his education to be put on hold. I needed Buddy to get caught up on his coursework and not worry about me. My parents were always supportive and being home would give me the support system I needed for now. I was determined to find a local law school and finish out my education. That was just the foundation of my plan. My plans could not be finalized until I found out how far along I was in my pregnancy and my due date.

I walked into the office of Dr. Reid, one of the best gynecologists in North Carolina. The office was plush. To my surprise, I was the only patient in the waiting room. The nurse called my name and I walked to the back. "Can my mom come?" I asked. The nurse said she would bring her back once the doctor gave permission. Shortly after I got settled in the examining room, the doctor walked in and introduced himself.

"So, Autumn, you just found out you are pregnant?"

"Yes." There I was, saying that word again.

He asked me a series of questions and I answered each one. I learned that it is not uncommon to be pregnant and still have your menstrual cycle. What was amazing was that I was not showing at all. Dr. Reid gave me a vaginal exam and an ultrasound. I was surprised to learn I was about five months pregnant. How could this be? I had no weight gained and only recently had started experiencing what they called "morning sickness" and exhaustion. The doctor, my mom, the nurse, and I heard the baby's heartbeat. Dr. Reid could not tell the sex of the baby yet, but it appeared to be a fat, round ball. I knew I could not return to Yale University or any other college in

January, being so far along in my pregnancy. I was determined to stay home, have my baby, and immediately return to school. I just could not figure out how to tell Buddy or when.

Buddy and I began to talk less and less, although I called more and more. By the time I reached six months it looked like I'd swallowed 20 basketballs. My dad kept asking if I was sure I wasn't having twins. "No, Dad, they only heard one heartbeat," I would reply.

My mom said, "That is going to be a big baby." My dad asked where Buddy was almost daily.

I would lie and say, "He wants to come but I need him to finish school. We have plans." At this stage of my life I had sprouted into a woman who was about to become a mother. I would often be concerned about what Buddy's reaction would be whenever he learned he was going to be a father. For now, I had to take full responsibility and raise my child to the best of my ability.

A New Leaf on Life

$\mathcal{S}$o much was happening so quickly in my life. I was about 8 ½ months pregnant, I still had not told Buddy he was going to be a father and our relationship seemed to have changed without my knowledge. We barely talked. I would always have to say, "I love you" first. Sometimes Buddy would act like he did not hear me and other times he would just hang up. I felt in my heart that Buddy and I did not share the same views of our future anymore. I began to pressure him by saying things like, "Are we still okay? Do you still love me? Are you hiding something from me? Are we still getting married?" Buddy would get so annoyed with me. I had never seen this side of him before. I got to a place where I stopped annoying him and asked God to reveal to me what was going on.

One night I awakened to someone constantly calling my phone. I could not figure out who it could be, and I prayed it was not an emergency. "Hello, is this Autumn?" the woman on the other line asked.

"Yes, this is Autumn." She introduced herself as Summer Nichols and questioned me about my relationship with Buddy. My mouth opened and my heart stopped. "I am his fiancée," I said before asking her how she got my telephone number. She told me she got it from Buddy. I did not believe her, but I could not confirm that without talking to Buddy. Summer told me that her and Buddy had been dating for six months and that they had plans to get married. How could this be? Buddy never broke it off with me. Hysterically, I hung up the phone. I had to talk to Buddy.

I constantly called Buddy for a week, day and night. I left messages asking him to call me. He would not answer the phone. I wanted to tell him about the baby with hopes it would change the situation.

One day my telephone rang. I looked at the caller ID and it was an unknown number. "Hello," I answered.

"Autumn, I am so sorry."

"Buddy, is it true? Are you in love with someone else?"

"Yes, Autumn."

I am so sorry, Autumn.

"How could you do this to me, Buddy?"

I heard slight whimpering.

"Bye, Buddy." *Should I call him back?* My heart said *no.*

I was so depressed in the days following that dreadful call. My mother, the psychologist, became my therapist. I never revealed to her that I had not informed Buddy about the baby.

Finally, it was my delivery day. I began having pains. We called Dr. Reid and he agreed to meet me at the hospital. I was so big, and my feet were so swollen that I needed help getting in the car. On the way to the hospital my water broke, and my mother said, "You will not be coming back home." It hurt so bad, I was crying and screaming. In between contractions I was wishing Buddy was with me. How could he be? I never told him I was pregnant. I made my decision and I knew I had to live with it. I made the choice to be a single parent and raise my baby with the help of my parents.

Within three hours, Dr. Reid was ready to deliver my baby. "Push," he continued to say. "I see the head. Here comes the baby." The baby came out and it was a girl. Then he said, "Wait, there is another baby. It is a boy." How could this be? I had twins. All the tests showed one baby and the ultrasound only captured one heartbeat. Dr. Reid explained that it was not uncommon for twins to embrace in the womb. This could be why only one heartbeat was heard. Dr. Reid told me they were fraternal twins, because identical twins are babies of the same sex. I could not believe how my life had transformed from the age of 16 to the age of 20. I had become a single mother with two babies.

"Where is Buddy?" my dad asked.

"Dad he has finals. He will be here."

Then my dad asked the infamous question: "What are your plans?"

"Dad, I am going to raise my kids, get my law degree, and work at your law practice." My parents supported my decision and promised to hire someone to assist with taking care of my children while I continued my studies. I registered to take summer classes at Elon University School of Law. I would have to commute 2 ½ hours each way on the days of my class because the school was 157 miles away from Black Mountain. I thought of relocating closer to the university, but I knew I needed my parents' support more than ever. I had not heard from Buddy, so I knew I had to try to forget about him for now.

It was the week before school and my parents had a beautiful gift for me, a new sports utility vehicle. I owed it to my children and my parents to fulfill my dreams and create a better life for them. My children did not ask to be here. I often wondered what I would tell them when they asked about their father. I was not sure yet.

So, my journey continued on a new path by way of Elon University. When I reached the school, it was not as big or glamorous as Yale University, but I was grateful. In fact, the class sizes were much smaller. I was not nervous, just anxious to continue what I had started. The classes were filled with more men than women, which I found to be the norm for law school. I was still wearing Buddy's engagement ring. I could not bring myself to take it off. Many of my classmates appeared to be interested in forming a relationship or dating, but I had developed trust issues. Buddy had moved on and I was raising our two children alone. I refused to lose my focus again. Also, I was feeling a sense of guilt with not being able to spend the time needed with my children.

One of my classmates asked if we could be study partners. He was not doing so well in the class. Herbert Fleming was his name. During the semesters, Herbert and I would talk on the phone for hours, just going over the coursework. It was helpful to me as well, and assisted me with memorizing torts, contracts, criminal law, civil procedure, and constitutional law. My dad's law firm was well rounded, and I would be a valuable additional no matter what type of law I chose to practice. I studied criminal law, but I wanted knowledge in various types of law. It was ambitious, but I always prided myself in being well prepared. After a few semesters Herbert began to take our relationship to another level by asking a lot of personal questions. I did not want to lead Herbert on, so I told him I was a single parent and had no interest in getting involved with anyone at this time. One day Herbert asked the heart wrenching question, "Where is their father?"

"It is complicated," was the only response I could give. The world is too small, and you never know who may know who. Three years came quickly and was approaching graduation. I was determined to immediately study for the bar exam.

Destiny sent me an invitation; she was getting married to her long-time boyfriend. We had kept in touch, so I called her to congratulate her. I could not bring myself to ask about Buddy. Although I wanted to badly, I was afraid of what I might learn with her response. Destiny was getting married in Gastonia, North Carolina. I nervously accepted the invite. I had no idea what I would say to Buddy if I saw him. Should I tell him about the babies? I guess the words would have to roll off my lips. It had been over four years since I'd gotten that dreadful call from Summer and almost five years since I'd seen Buddy.

On the day of the wedding I made it a point to look glamorous. I was so nervous that I contemplated not attending, but I could not do that to Destiny. I was still wearing the engagement ring. I never took it off. When I arrived at the church, I refused to look around at the guests. I hurried to find a seat and remained looking forward. As they were going through the order of service, the strangest thing happened. They were calling my name, and then I noticed my name was on the program for me to pray for the couple. That meant that I would have to face the audience and if Buddy was in attendance, he would know that I was there. What would he say? What would be his reaction? Here I was again, overthinking things. Buddy might not have even be here. I could not really say I was surprised because oftentimes Destiny would call for me to pray for her and her family. All my friends were aware that I was the person who was called upon to pray in my grandfather's church. I stood up and walked to the microphone. I did a quick glance over the guests in the congregation and to my surprise I did not see Buddy, but I spotted his parents among the guests. I prayed from my heart and prayed blessings upon the couple. People must have felt it came from my heart because when I finished, I heard the applause.

At the end of the wedding Buddy's parents called me over to them. We all greeted each other with hugs. I could not resist the urge to ask, "How is Buddy?"

"Buddy is well," his father said. I asked if he graduated and his parents said that he did and that he was going to begin working at their practice after his honeymoon. Time stopped, or was it just my heart?

"Oh. Buddy got married?" I asked, trying to keep my composure.

"Yes, he is on his honeymoon. That is the only reason he is not here," Buddy's mother said. Then they asked me about my family. They still had no idea my children existed. If I told them they would be disappointed and would rush to call Buddy, which would inter-fere with his happiness. I just could not do that to him or me. I knew that type of life interference would change the way he felt about me forever.

"Did you graduate?" Buddy's father asked.

"Yes, I am studying for the bar," I quickly answered. I had to get out and away from them. I felt the tears about to fall. I refused to cry in front of them. I knew that would raise suspicion and leave me open for a lot of additional questions that I was not ready to answer. Then Buddy's father said, "We will tell Buddy we saw you and that you and your family are well."

"Thank you," I said. On my way home I pulled over on the side of the road and could not stop the tears. I cried profusely. I imme-diately prayed and asked God to please come see about me and heal the pain of me not telling Buddy about our twins, Matthew Buddy Dorsey, III and Destiny Kia Dorsey. Yes, I named our son after his father without his family even knowing that either of them existed. I was in so much pain. I made up in my mind that I needed God, so I decided to go to church for service.

My children and I went to church and on a normal day I would just sit in a pew. I was in so much pain, I asked one of the members to keep an eye out for my children and I proceeded to the front of the church and kneeled at the altar. I cried and cried. "God, please help me. Please forgive me. Please make this right for me. God, please help me to get over this pain and move on." I said this prayer and pled to God almost daily at church and at home. I had to come to the realization that Buddy had moved on and it was only fair that I do the same.

I finally passed the bar exam. My family and I celebrated. My parents were just as happy as I was. I said, "I can finally rest." That night I had a dream and I knew it was God, although I could not see Him. He said, "Preach my word." When I woke up, I looked around the room because it did not appear that I was having a dream. It appeared so real. The very next morning I called my grandfather because I knew he would be the person that could give me some clarity about my dream. I told my grandfather the entire dream. He remained silent. Finally, he said, "Meet with me this afternoon at the church."

I got the twins dressed, went to the church, and met with my grandfather. My grandmother was there to care for the twins so my grandfather and I could talk privately. My grandfather took my hands and prayed. Then he asked, "Will you answer God's call?"

"I am compelled to say yes to God," I replied. My grandfather had tears in his eyes as he looked through me. There was a certain glean in his eyes that was beyond a normal stare. I believed my grandfather was so proud and happy that his 24-year-old granddaughter accepted the call of God. I asked my grandfather what God wanted me to do now. "Go to Bible school," he said. *What?* I was not ready for that. I expected to pray, fast, or even attend church more. *Go to Bible school* hit me like a ton of bricks. I had just finished school.

"When do I have time to go to Bible school and raise two children?" I asked him.

"You have the time," he said. "You went to school and took care of your kids while you were in law school. You drove five hours a day to get your law degree. Nothing will compare to your degree in studying God's word." I agreed and knew this was something I had to do. I knew it was not my grandfather talking, but God Himself. Therefore, I was obedient and signed up to take Bible classes online at Grace Christian University. My children had sacrificed enough, so online was the best thing to do for all of us. Five-year-old children needed their mother. I had adopted a new leaf on this life.

I really enjoyed my classes. Each class I learned more and more. I was virtually meeting people from various places in the United States of America. These were people whose path I may have never crossed in this life, but online classes afforded me the opportunity to have extended friends in different cities. One of the requirements of each class was that you had to introduce yourself to your colleagues. Some of people I recognized their names because we had classes together and some people, we were virtually meeting for the first time. Some students would place their picture on the screen, and some would use something other than their image to display on their profile. I displayed one of the best pictures I owned. One of the most astonishing things for me was the amazing ministry experience of so many of my classmates. I was a novice in this world. When I got to my fifth class of my biblical studies, I posted what I always posted. I stated my name, my education, my profession, and the names of my beautiful children. Of course, I had to brag that God had blessed me with twin children. This class was different than the rest because there seemed to be a lot more people registered in this class. There were over 30 people, while previous classes had only about ten people registered. The day after I posted my introduction, I went into the discussion to welcome all my fellow colleagues who had posted their introductions. I also wanted to respond to any students or the instructor if they posted something about my introduction. As I was going through the list, I noticed a name that stood out, Matthew Buddy Dorsey, II. I literally froze. This could not be the same person I knew. I grew nervous and my heart had to have stopped beating because I could not feel anything. When I looked at the profile picture, it was just a symbol of the cross. This person never stated anything about their hometown, family, or profession. All he wrote was, "My name is Matthew Buddy Dorsey, II. I accepted the call of God in my life and I am humbled by the experience. I am looking forward to learning about God's word with you and excited about what God is doing in my life. I am looking for great things to happen and miracles to unfold." This was too much of a coincidence. It had to be the father of my children. What was I going to do now? All I knew is that I felt that my past decisions, secrets, and mistakes were now coming to the surface. I tell you this, miracles were unfolding, and it would cause Buddy and I to embark on a new leaf in life.

Beginning to Appreciate the Beauty

Whoever this Matthew Buddy Dorsey, II was, he welcomed me and we never exchanged any other messages. It was possible that there could be several men with the same name in the United States. Each class was 12 weeks long and all this drama had occurred during the first week. I had not heard anything from the man I presumed to be my children's father. Perhaps I had overreacted. He never stated the one liner he gave to many: "My friends call me Buddy."

During the tenth week of class, there was a knock at my door. I looked out of the window to see who was paying my family and I a visit. We were not expecting anyone. When I looked out the window, I noticed it was Buddy, his father, and his mother. Buddy looked the same, just a little more mature. He had grown facial hair. Why were they outside my parents' door? Perhaps for a friendly visit. However, the expressions on their faces made me nervous. I did not feel I was overreacting after all. I had literally dropped breathing.

"Who is at the door?" my mom yelled from the kitchen.

"I got it, Mom." I opened the door with a friendly smile. Buddy asked if they could come in and I stepped aside so they could enter. There was no time to hide the children, who were sitting at the dining room table doing their homework. Besides, how could I hide two five-year-old children. When Buddy walked in the door, I noticed how his eyes were examining the entire house. Was he looking for pictures or the actual children? Either way, I knew he was looking to see something. Buddy froze when he spotted my son and my daughter sitting at the dining room table. I never realized how much the children resembled Buddy and his father. Buddy was directly in front of the sofa and his parents were right beside him. Buddy sat down and his parents sat down beside him on the sofa. They kept staring at the children. My mom entered the living room from the kitchen, and, with impeccable timing, my dad walked into the house from the front door. What was I going to say? I never told Buddy about the children. I disobeyed my dad and my lies were about to surface. I began to pray silently with my eyes wide open.

Buddy looked at me and asked, "Are these my children?" with tears in his eyes.

Immediately my dad responded, "What you mean are these your children? You know they are your children."

I had to quickly intervene. "Dad, please let me answer. I never told Buddy I was pregnant." My dad appeared shocked. I began to cry. My dad could never handle me crying. I looked at Buddy and tears were streaming down his eyes. I looked at his parents and they were crying also, along with my mom.

"How could you let me not be in their lives? Why would you do this, Autumn?" I apologized and explained that I thought I was doing the right thing, but either way I recognized I was wrong.

I called our children. "Matthew and Destiny, come give your father and grandparents a big hug." The twins had great hearts. They ran and leaped into Buddy's arms. Now everyone in the room was crying, even my dad.

After several minutes and lots of hugs, Buddy asked, "Can I speak with you in private?" I walked toward the front door and headed to the porch. Buddy looked at me with such disappointment. "What do we do now?" he asked. "Where do we go from here? How is this going to be handled?" The questions were coming so quickly, I had to have time to process the answers.

I said, "The first thing you should do is discuss all of this with your wife. I will be very flexible and the three of us can come up with a plan to schedule visits, and when everyone is ready, we will have the twins begin to spend some time with the two of you alone." After all, that was the right thing to do. Buddy had a wife and I could not see myself disrespecting her or excluding her. That is the way I would want to be treated if I were her. Then Buddy said five words that almost knocked me off my feet.

"I am no longer married." I dared not ask what happened, but Buddy proceeded to willingly provide me with an explanation. "I thought she was pregnant, and I wanted to do the right thing." I stared with amazement and disbelief. "I wanted to reach out to you, but my parents said they saw a ring on your finger, so I did not want to interfere with your happiness." That sounded too familiar. I lifted my hand and Buddy immediately recognized it was the ring he had given me. Both of our eyes began to water. I wanted to hug him, but I dared not be the first to do so.

"I never took it off," I said. It was an era of my life I never wanted to forget, even though I decided to move on." Move on where? I never even had another date. I was building a wall between Buddy and I to be used for protection. Suddenly, we embraced, and Buddy lightly pushed me away.

"I never stopped loving you. It is obvious you feel the same," said Buddy. I saw the entire situation was moving swiftly to the past. I asked if we could talk later, and we agreed to go back in with our families and catch up later. Before Buddy and his family's departure, he had me agree to meet him with the children the very next day.

We decided to meet at a park for a picnic. While the children were playing alone, we had an opportunity to talk. It appeared that Buddy and I were both studying for the ministry to become more active in the churches we attended. I asked Buddy about his feelings after reading my post.

"I read the post at least ten times. I was speechless and could not internalize that I had twins out there that I knew nothing about. I just could not process the idea and did not know how to handle the situation. That is why it took me so many weeks to arrive at your parents' home. I did not know if you still lived there, but I knew they would tell me the truth and arrange a meeting for me."

"Buddy, I wanted to tell you so many times. I know the type of man you are and when you told me you were behind in your course-work, I knew you would drop everything and come to me. Then I decided to tell you when the semester ended for you. It was then that I got the call from Summer Nichols...I still remember her name."

"That is who I married," Buddy said. Suddenly, the pain of the past came rushing back. The vision of reconciliation between Buddy and I was blurred by the pain that Buddy caused me through his lies and his broken promises. It was at that moment I decided to just remain friends.

Buddy admired my willingness to do it alone. He assured me that he was going to step up as a father and that I did not have to do it. I continued to emphasize that we would still be friends. He felt heartbroken over not being able to parent his children and over his marriage.

"I felt like a failure," he said. Marriage should be until death separates you." He revealed that he would not have gotten married if he knew it would not last. At first, I was getting my feelings involved. He promised to marry me and fell in love with someone else. Then I realized that whatever was meant to be would be. To my surprise, he said his parents warned him about his ex-wife and told him to wait. Buddy, being a perfect gentleman, stressed that he thought she was pregnant. That let me know that if he knew I was pregnant he would have come back for all the wrong reasons. Hearing him speak gave me even more confidence that I did the right thing by not telling him. Again, I asked about the telephone call from Summer. He continued to apologize and was sorrowful that I had to go through that, especially while I was pregnant. The entire meeting was full of apologies and regrets.

I learned that Buddy worked in his parents' medical practice. I was glad to hear he had graduated with honors. He felt bad that I did not get the opportunity to graduate from Yale. I assured him I had no regrets. I graduated top of my class and was working at my dad's law firm. "Dreams are full of details, yet they never outline what all is involved in reaching the goal," I said. Buddy just laughed. We were laughing like friends. I was so happy about that.

It had been four months of semi-family dinners and outings, and now the twins were going to stay with Buddy alone. They would be away for two weeks to bond with him and his family, without me. I missed them already and they were only walking toward the car. Buddy and I were still in Bible school. During class times, if the twins were with me, Buddy would sometimes send a private message asking how our babies were. When they were with him, he would just seem so proud to be their dad. His words would make me blush, but I knew we could not pick up from where we left off. Co-parenting was working and I wanted our relationship to bloom from there. We were no longer teenagers or struggling students. We had real responsibilities and obligations. I had finally taken the ring off. When Buddy first noticed it was removed from my hand, he displayed a strange look on his face. When he finally got up the heart to ask me if I took it off, I asked him if he wanted it back.

He said, "No, I gave that to you as a token of my love for you." I laughed and changed the conversation. Perhaps I was still hurt and carrying around some resentment from how our relationship unfolded. I did not feel I could trust him again.

Men were getting bolder and bolder. During the discussion forums, fellow colleagues were asking me out on dates. Buddy was witnessing all of it. We were out to dinner with the twins when Buddy asked, "Are you dating?"

"Not yet," I responded, "Are you?"

" I do not have time. My life is full of work and our kids right now." It was a beautiful thing to hear "our kids." My life was blossoming. Buddy and I had become good friends and our children finally had their father.

Start of Blooming Season

*I*t was the day Buddy and I were both graduating from Bible school. The graduation was being held in Charlotte, North Carolina. We both opted not to go but to get our degrees mailed to us. Time flew by so quickly. I had preached at my grandfather's church several times and was placed as head of the women's ministry. So many doors had opened for me and I was preaching all over North Carolina. Buddy and the children accompanied me many times. It was always strange explaining who Buddy was, especially with the twins yelling mom and dad. The twins were now eight years old. Buddy became assistant pastor of the church he and his family attended in Gastonia. I preached there for two of their women's day services. Our children were so blessed. Buddy asked to take me out a few times, but I declined. However, we were always going to dinner with the twins.

Buddy believed his church was pressuring him into getting married. He was one of the most eligible bachelors in the church. He was a doctor, handsome, single, and a true man of God. Every single woman in the church wanted him. Whenever I would visit, several women would yell his name to get his attention. I would just smile. I felt Buddy was playing it safe this time around and was mindful of who he got involved with. Every now and then he would ask, "You still have my ring?" It droves him crazy that I no longer wore it and oftentimes I did not respond when he asked that question. My dad, the bold one of the family, asked me every so often when me and

Buddy were getting back together. I would simply say, "Only when God says so." I learned when you put God into the equation, people tend to back off.

It was the Sunday that Buddy was officially being ordained as the assistant pastor of his church. He asked if the twins and I would attend. Buddy had always been so supportive and a great dad, I felt obligated to go and support him during this glorious occasion. I just prayed that I would not give people the wrong idea or impression of our relationship. I did not want anyone to think we were anything outside of friends and co-parents. I had to make sure our children looked extra nice. Matthew had on a sharp suit and Destiny had on a beautiful dress. These two little people represented the Dorsey and French clan; people of excellence and class. Of course, I refused to not spare any expense on my look for the service.

When we reached the church entrance, I saw Buddy's eyes plastered to the door. The moment we stepped into the church, he was signaling to the usher to sit us by his parents. As I scanned the congregation, I noticed a mixture of our college friends and women who were wondering where I was going. Everyone was looking at me smiling and I made sure to return the gesture. I assumed Buddy told them about our family arrangement--man, woman and twins.

The service was beautiful, and I was so happy for Buddy. He called the twins and his parents up. I was not offended, because I had no business up there. I was not his wife, fiancée, or girlfriend. I was just proud to see my children so happy. A wonderful reception followed the service. Buddy had reserved a place at the head of his table for the twins and I. His parents were sitting there too. I was wondering what was going on. I felt honored, but I felt out of place. Buddy and I laughed the entire event. He got caught whispering to me about different things or we would just laugh about our children.

One thing those kids could do was eat a lot. They were so small so we could not figure out where all the food was going.

The event lasted for a very long time. I may be exaggerating but it seemed like thousands of people were giving speeches and gifting Buddy for his spiritual promotion. It was late, and the twins and I were so tired. As we were preparing to drive about an hour and a half back to Black Mountain, Buddy pled for us to stay at his home. I had never been to his home. He no longer lived with his parents. I easily agreed because I knew the roads were dark and my children and I were exhausted. I was especially tired because of all the food I ate. Buddy put the children in his car, and I followed him to his house. It looked beautiful and spacious from the outside. When I entered through the door, the home was beautifully decorated. I did not expect anything less.

"Make yourself at home," Buddy said. I will put the kids to bed." A few minutes later, he yelled down the stairs for me to come see their rooms. I walked up the steps and each one of our children had beautifully decorated rooms filled with toys. He showed me the beautiful room I would be sleeping in. It had a private bathroom. "Would you like some tea or coffee?" Buddy asked.

"Yes," I said, thinking it would help to dissolve all that food I had eaten. He handed me a big shirt to sleep in. I thanked him. In this moment of togetherness and experiencing his attentiveness I felt I could love him again. "Is everything okay?" I asked him. The flood gates of love were opening again.

Buddy said, "I know I said this before and did not follow through on the promise, but I do not care how long it takes to win you back. I am going to marry you." We both took a deep breath. "I will not pressure you and God will let us both know the right time,"

he continued. Then there was silence. I wanted so bad to say something that could speed up the process. My insides were jumping.
"I will do it your way this time around," proclaimed Buddy. These
words ignited my passion. I leaned over and touched his hand.

"You just say the word, give me a date, and name the place,"
I said. "I never loved anyone else but you." The words rolled out of
my mouth without any hesitation. It was the beginning of our lives
coming into bloom.

CHAPTER 6

The Branch

S itting in my office on the 14th floor, I felt a sense of accomplishment. I had come a long way from being that 16-year-old girl who went to college, graduated with honors, became a single parent of twins, and passed the North Carolina bar exam. As I gazed out of the window all I could see was God's beautiful creation. I felt like jumping up and yelling, "I survived!" I survived disappointment, I survived heartbreak, and I established a stable home for my children. "Let me calm down," I said silently to myself. I was too excited. It seemed I always got excited when I felt I had everything figured out, only to discover that life always had surprises in store.

"Hey, Autumn!" my brother Adam yelled as he walked into my office without knocking on the door.

"Adam, please knock on my door before you come in. I never barge in your office, "I replied jokingly. My brother Adam is my parents' second oldest child and my oldest brother. We both worked at my dad's law firm. Now my dad had two of his children working alongside him. Adam majored in contractual law and I majored in criminal law.

Adam always acted as if he was older than me. "Autumn, Dad wants to take us to lunch if you are free," said Adam.

"Of course, I would love to go to lunch with Dad," I replied.

"Oh, you don't want to go to lunch with your big brother?" asked Adam.

"Adam, I am older than you. I love you, baby bro," I stated as I was rising from my seat to go hug my brother. "I would like nothing more than to eat with you." Adam blushed as the words were coming out of my mouth.

In walked my dad. "Are you ready, Autumn and Adam?" he asked, and with cheerful hearts we all walked out of the office and went to my dad's favorite spot.

Whenever my dad went into Ms. Lucy's café, he always got her personal attention. Ms. Lucy yelled, "Hi, Attorney Adam and family, sit where you want."

My dad smiled and we all went to his favorite table in the corner. He turned and looked at Adam and I and said, "I am so proud of the two of you." My brother and I both smiled. "The law firms board has decided to open a new office in Weaverville, North Carolina. That is about 27 minutes from Black Mountain." My dad made it clear that the firm was beginning to get a lot of clients from Weaverville and the firm's representation was growing. There was a huge client base in Weaverville. My dad asked my brother and I if we would be interested in working at the new location. He made it clear that we did not have to relocate if we did not want to, but he would like for at least one of us to work from that location. Then my dad turned in my direction and said, "Autumn, discuss this with Buddy. I know the two of you will be getting married at some point. You need Buddy to agree with your decision." I was kind of confused because Buddy and I had just officially started dating and he had not proposed. However, I knew my dad was right. After all, our children would be impacted by my decision and it could affect all our futures.

My brother Adam was dating a woman who was about five years older than him and four years older than me. My parents were quite fond of her. She was a circuit court judge in our county. Judge Ashley Weatherbe was a beautiful, intelligent, and charismatic woman. She did not even look her age. In fact, she looked younger than Adam. My dad would always throw out hints to Adam by saying, "Don't let this one get away." I would laugh because my dad is known for telling you how he feels. I could not read my brother's silent response, but I knew he loved her. All Adam would talk about is Ashley and she would accompany him to every family event. The two of them were inseparable.

As lunch was ending, my dad was sharing with my brother and I his family expectations, or at least his knowledge of the career paths chosen by his seven children. My dad was grateful for the fact that Adam and I chose to follow in his footsteps, but he knew the buck stopped there. My second younger brother, Robert, was going to medical school. Robert reminded everyone of this whenever he was asked if he was going to college. My third younger brother, Jerry, had decided to follow our mom's career path and become a psychologist. What was surprising was that our fourth and fifth brothers were musically inclined. They could sing, had an ear for music, and could play almost any instrument. Kirk and Dennis were unofficial twins. They did everything together, despite them being one year apart. They both often stated they were going to seminary and would become very active in Christian ministry. They traveled with our grandfather on many occasions and he was grooming them to take over the church choir on a full-time basis. Our youngest brother, Daniel, was undecided as to what he was going to do. He had a beautiful voice and was determined to pursue a career in secular music. I could sing, but my brothers were very gifted in singing. I was gifted to pray and preach God's word. My dad was quite sure that all his children were not going to choose his career path.

All my dad's children were dating except for the three young-est. I was dating Buddy, Adam was dating Ashley, Jerry was dating our neighbor's daughter, Emily, and Robert had a girlfriend who we never met, but he was always talking to her on the phone. I did not know if any of us were quite ready for marriage, but we all had dreams with the determination that we would obtain those dreams in this lifetime. I was already a mother so if anyone should have been ready it should have been me. I just could not settle. I had to love the man. Buddy was the only one I had ever loved. I tried many times to move on, but my heart just would not allow me. Even when he was married to Summer, my love for him would not die. It could be the fact he was my first boyfriend, my first love, and the father of my children. I wanted to be his wife, but I had to wait on the right time. Divorce was not an option for me.

I was quite active in my grandfather's church. I had even set up a free law clinic. Many people needed legal information and some needed appropriate representation. I had arranged for lawyers to volunteer a few hours per month and offer pro bono services in every area of the law to those in dire need. I saw the need to pro-vide the community with this type of legal service, but I could not afford to overload my schedule. I had to spend alone time with God, alone time with my 10-year-old twins, time with Buddy, and I was obligated to effectively represent the clients whose cases I was hired to defend. Also, I could not neglect the women's ministry. There are only seven days in a week, with 168 hours in that timespan, and some *me* time had to be included in those days so I could regroup. My life was truly full, yet my life was so rewarding. It had sprouted buds after all the planting, now the branch was growing as it proceeded forward into the future.

Arrangements Jakes Organization

I had finally bought me a house. I felt it was time to move out of my parents' house. It was not as big as Buddy's, his parents, or my parent's home, but it had three bedrooms with four bathrooms, a two-car garage, a front and back porch, a balcony outside of the master bedroom and it sat on an acre of land. The kids loved the house. The most shocking thing for them was that we did not have a housekeeper. Therefore, they were given a chore list. My parents, Buddy's parents, and Buddy all had a housekeeper. Despite all the help, I wanted my children to be responsible. The expressions they had on their faces showed me they wanted to run away back to their grandparents' house or with their dad. I needed to raise a responsible man and a responsible woman, so chores it was.

My telephone continued to ring as I was in the kitchen preparing dinner. The twins were staying with Buddy for the weekend. Although they ate a lot, they were very picky when it came to eating. I wanted to prepare some home cooked food for them. "Hello," I answered.

"Autumn, we are about ten minutes away," said Buddy.

"I cooked. Would you like to take a plate or sit with us?" I asked.

"I will sit and eat with you, if you do not mind," replied Buddy.

Mine, I thought to myself. *After you eat, you can stay here forever.* I dreamed of that moment. "Okay, Buddy. I cooked chicken, sweet potatoes, vegetables, and corn bread."

"Great," Buddy replied. He appeared to be as excited as I was.

By the time Buddy and the twins arrived, the table was set, and the food was served. We all sat down to eat dinner and Buddy blessed the food. It was amazing to have the experience of us sitting down to a homecooked meal as a family. We often went out to eat. It could have just been the fact that I was sitting down in my new home. Of course, I had lived in a dorm before, but I'd never had my own house, decorated the way I liked and with my own furniture. Although the twins were ten years old, I still fixed their plates so they would not make a mess.

"How was your weekend?" asked Buddy.

"My weekend was great. I missed my babies," I replied. Buddy and I both smiled. The twins looked at me like they wanted to say, " We are not babies," however, I raised them to always be mindful of your words and who you are talking to. That is old school upbringing. It was a family value that I cherished and one that has helped me to overcome many obstacles in this life. Matthew and Destiny began to express how much fun they had with Buddy and his family. Destiny seemed to always agree with everything Matthew would say.

I noticed Buddy was just staring at me. Then he said, "Autumn what are you doing tomorrow?"

"I do not have anything special scheduled," I replied.

"Do you think your mom would mind watching the twins while I take you to dinner? There are a few things I really need to discuss with you," said Buddy.

"I don't know but let me call her and check to see," I said to Buddy. "Do you mind if I call right now," I asked Buddy.

"Of course not. Please do," he said. So, I picked up my cell phone and let the phone ring until my mom answered.

"Mom, how are you? Did I catch you at a good time?" I asked my mom.

"Hi, daughter. It is always a good time when you call. How are you? Is everything okay?"

"Tell your mom I said hi," Buddy said.

"Yes, Mom. Buddy wants to take me to dinner tomorrow. Do you mind if the twins come over? I will send them with their pajamas and church clothes just in case I get home late. Is that okay?"

My mom was so excited. "Of course, my grandchildren can come whenever."

"Thanks, Mom. I love you. Buddy said hi."

"Hi, Buddy!" my mom yelled. My family's feelings for Buddy changed drastically after they learned he did not desert me and that I had keep my pregnancy a secret. My family loved Buddy. They were probably praying as hard as I was that we would get married.

"I will be here to pick you up at 5:00 PM if that is okay," stated Buddy.

"That is fine," I replied.

My mom called back. "I have to go to the store in the morning so I will pick them up in the morning if that is okay," she said.

"Sure, Mom. I will have them up and ready," I replied. "Thank you so much, Mom. I love you," I said as we were ending the call.

After Buddy left, I began to get into in my head with thoughts, concerns, and worries about what Buddy could possibly want to talk to me about. He seemed so serious. This would give me the opportunity to talk to Buddy about the conversation I had with my dad that involved the new law office, which would require me to work and possibly relocate to Weaverville. It could be a marriage proposal because we had officially began dating. *I better go to bed and get a good night's sleep*, I thought. I tossed and turned all night.

The next thing I knew, my alarm was ringing. It was 8:00 AM. When my mom said she would be there in the morning, it could be as early as 10:00 AM. My mom was an early riser. I wanted the twins to have eaten breakfast and be dressed and ready to go when my mom arrived.

"Good morning, Matthew and Destiny. It will be ready by time you are out of the shower and dressed," I yelled from the first floor. "Please pack you some pajamas and take you an outfit to wear to church tomorrow," I said to them.

"Okay, Mom," replied Matthew and Destiny. I fixed them a hearty breakfast and they were ready. My mom would be arriving soon because she had to go to the market. My younger brothers lived at home and then my two children were coming. They all ate a lot of food and my mom was probably going to stock up for them. She spoiled my children because presently they were her only grandchildren.

After about 20 minutes of cleaning up, my mom was coming in the door with her key.

"Daughter, are they ready?" asked my mom. The twins exited the kitchen yelling, "Grandma!" They probably were excited to get over there because they did not have to do too much. My mom and I embraced.

"Give your mother a hug and a kiss. We are leaving," my mom told the twins.

They ran to hug and kiss me. "See you later, Mom," they yelled, leaving out the door with my mom. I decided to go back to bed and get some more rest. Buddy would be here between 4:00 PM and 4:30 PM, although, he said 5:00 PM. He was like my mom, always early. Buddy was another early bird.

I put on a fancy dress and heels. I had my hair stylist come over to do my hair and makeup. I wore makeup daily, but I needed a special application. Susan was a good friend and a stylist to the stars. I was hoping she was in town. When I called, she answered and always was willing to render assistance. She was pricey, but well worth every dollar. I called in the cavalry because I wanted to feel good inside and out.

Like clockwork, there was a knock at the door. I knew it was Buddy. I was not expecting anyone, and it was 4:27 PM. When I looked out the window, there was Buddy standing there looking so handsome. He had on a black suit with a brilliantly colorful tie and handkerchief. We were coordinated because I wore my sexy black dress, heels, jewelry, and of course makeup to highlight the entire outfit. When I opened the door, Buddy was speechless.

"You...you look beautiful," he stuttered. Buddy could not take his eyes off me and I could not take my eyes off him. "Are you ready?" he asked.

"Yes, I'm ready," I replied as I was closing the door behind me. Buddy reached for my hand and led me to his car. He was always the perfect gentleman and he opened the car door for me and closed the door after I got in safely.

Buddy seemed so nervous as we were driving to the place he had made reservations for. I had no clue as to where we were going. Before I could ask, Buddy was taking me to a dinner hosted by one of his medical colleagues. It was held in a mansion. They valeted Buddy's car and we walked to the front door. When we walked into the event, I was confident that I was dressed perfectly for it. People seem to stare at Buddy and I when we walked in. Was it because Buddy used to bring his ex-wife or maybe he had always come solo? Either way, I was here on his arm and I did not care about anything else. I met so many important people in the medical profession from all over the United States. I asked Buddy if his dad was in attendance, but he said, "No, I am here to represent my dad." Buddy introduced me to many people. When he first said, "This is Autumn, my fiancée and the mother of my twins," I was surprised, but I refused to look surprised. There was no ring on my finger, but I gathered that Buddy had his reasons.

"We are not going to be here too long because I really need to talk to you," said Buddy. I was really confused. I knew Buddy did not bring me here to talk so I was a little anxious to hear what was so important. The food was great, the décor was breathtaking, and the man whose company I was in was worth it all. It was just not the atmosphere for a serious conversation. An hour had passed. "We will be leaving in a half an hour," Buddy whispered to me, "Is that okay with you?"

"Yes, that is fine with me," I replied, "Whatever you decide." out. "Is it okay to go to my house?" he asked once we had gotten in the car. "Just for privacy and then I will take you home."

I wanted to ask. "For what?" We both had accepted the call of God and there could be no fooling around unless we were married. But I trusted Buddy, so I simply said, "No problem." Then my mind started to wonder if this would be one of those goodbye conversations. My breathing felt like it wanted to stop, and my heartrate was rising. I wanted to yell, "Would you please just tell me what it is?"

"Are you okay?" he asked.

I said, "Yes."

Then he spoke most confronting words: "It is something good." I could finally relax.

We finally arrived at Buddy's home. He opened the door and we headed toward his family room. We sat on the patio and Buddy asked if I wanted some tea, coffee, water, or juice. I asked for a cup of coffee. I had to make sure I was fully awake to hear every word of this serious conversation that was some good news. My insides were screaming, "Buddy, would you sit down and talk?" Yet I played it cool. Buddy brought back the drinks and sat directly in front of me.

"Autumn, I love you," he began. "I no longer want to live without waking up to you." I was frozen and I felt myself ready to faint. I realized I had to hold on to get all the details and see where this conversation was going. "I no longer want to be a co-parent; I want to be a full-time parent with you. I know I hurt you in the past and I will forever be sorrowful for my actions. I pray you have fully forgiven me. I want to marry you. It does not have to be a big wedding and I do not want to wait any longer than six months. I am satisfied with just our families here," said Buddy. Then he knelt in front of me with a diamond ring that looked to be two to three carats. "Will you please do me the honor and marry me?" asked Buddy.

With tears streaming down both of our faces, I said, "Yes, yes, yes!"

"Nothing will stop this from happening this time. I need you and our children." We embraced and it seemed as though neither of us wanted to let go. A few minutes later Buddy was texting. I felt it was an inappropriate time to be doing so.

"Who are you texting?" I asked.

"My parents, your parents, our children, and my pastor." It seems everyone knew he was going to propose. Now it made sense why my dad said to me at lunch to make sure I asked Buddy because we would be getting married at some point and it could affect our future. Buddy had asked my father for my hand in marriage. Now it was my turn.

"Buddy, my dad asked my brother Adam and I to relocate our office or home to Weaverville, North Carolina. Apparently, the firm's business is expanding in that area and the board decided to open a law firm there," I stated. Buddy did not think about the impact before he replied, "I will live wherever you want to live, as long as you are there. Just be my wife. If I have to commute, I will." Was Buddy saying he would move to Black Mountain? I do not know, but I knew I would follow his lead in this situation.

"If you move to Black Mountain what about the church where you are assistant pastor?"

"I already spoke to my pastor and your grandfather. Your grandfather told me he would love to have me take the pastor position and that he would move into the overseer position," said Buddy. I was shocked by now. Then I asked the single most important question of our lives: "What did God say to do?" Buddy could not answer that question. "Buddy, do you mind if we pray about all this and we do whatever God tells us or leads us to do? We can ask our moms to coordinate a nice wedding in one of their yards or in the back of your house. All I know is that this will serve as the baby shower I never had and the day when I finally marry the love of my life." I cried with a sigh of relief. I knew in my heart that I belonged with Buddy. Blossoming in this life is a process that can require heartaches, disappointments, and tears. Yet I was learning that you should allow your life to become organized with God's will. And only then will you line up with your destiny.

Seeds Maturing

*H*e had decided to move into Buddy's house in Gastonia, North Carolina for now. My dad gave me the luxury of working from home at least three days a week and reporting to the office the other two days, unless I had a scheduled trial. Buddy, on the other hand, had to continue to take care of his patients. That was an oath he had taken as a doctor. It appeared to be more feasible for us to remain close to his practice. We were trying to figure out whether to sell my home or just keep it in the family. That hadn't quite been decided yet.

Our wedding day was quickly approaching. Our moms decided to have the wedding at Buddy's parents' home. We invited 50 guests to our wedding. The guests were mainly our families. It took three months to plan and here I was about to be Mrs. Autumn Dorsey. The bridesmaids were our daughter, Destiny, my college friends, April and Destiny (who I named my daughter after), Buddy's only sister, Jessica, my brother Adam's girlfriend, Ashley, and my cousin, Spring. Buddy's groomsmen consisted of our son, Matthew and my six brothers. My grandfather performed the ceremony along with Buddy's pastor. Our parents were so excited. The wedding was well organized, and Buddy and I are overly excited, right along with our children.

I found the most beautiful gown and shoes. My mom and I were on our way to a fancy bridal shop. I had decided not to wear white, but rather off white. I was already a mother and I was raised that you do not wear white if you have children before the wedding. I was okay with that. I did not care what color I wore, if I was marrying Buddy. As we approached the bridal shop, we spotted the most beautiful dress I ever saw in the window. The design of the dress even stopped my mom in her tracks. It was what people call eggshell white and it appeared to be designed for a princess.

My mom said, "Autumn, let's go have you try that dress on. It looks like it is your size." I could not get the door open fast enough. A lady who worked in the shop approached us and introduced herself as Nancy.

"What size is this dress in the window? Can my daughter try it on?"

"Sure," Nancy said. She took the dress off the mannequin and led me back to the dressing room. When I put the dress on it was perfect in size and perfect in length. My mom and I both cried because it looked so beautiful. It was as if the dress was designed specifically for me. Nancy said, "There are some brand new shoes over there that you may like." My mom and I proceeded to the shoe section. Then were lined up by size. I walked over the section that was labeled 8 ½ M. There were the most beautiful shoes I had ever seen sitting in a box. I tried them on, and they were comfortable and fit perfect. I had learned when you wear heels, it is best to get shoes that are comfortable.

My mom and I took the shoes to the counter. Nancy was ringing everything up. The dress had a $2,500 price tag on it and the shoes had a $299 price tag on the box. "This is going to cost about $1,000," I whispered.

"Don't worry about the cost," my mom said, "That is your dress and shoes."

"That will be $70," Nancy said. My mom and I looked at each other.

"How much do we owe you?" I asked.

"$70."

"Pay the woman, Autumn," my mom said. I put my card back in my wallet and handed Nancy $70. I tried to give Nancy a tip, but she said she could not accept it.

"Continue to let God bless you," Nancy said. As my mom and I were going out the door another salesclerk congratulated us on our purchase. Then she said, "Did you see all the bridesmaid dresses and shoes?" My mom and I did an about face and went to a rack that had all these pale yellow dresses. We knew it could not be a coincidence. Buddy and I talked about pale yellow for the dresses and the cummerbunds. I began to call all our bridal party and get their dress and shoe sizes. We purchased seven of the dresses and they had the shoes to match. Each of the women in my wedding could fit a pair of shoes, except my daughter, Destiny. The total came to $375. Each woman in the bridal party owed me $54. My mom and I ran to the car in case Nancy or the other saleswoman would try to get the dresses and shoes back.

When we got home, I made arrangements for every bridesmaid to come to my mom's house and try her dress and shoes on. My mom and I could not stop looking at each other. Bridesmaid after bridesmaid came out and looked so beautiful in their dress and shoes. My daughter Destiny was the only one that needed shoes. We sent all the dresses for dry cleaning. I asked each bridesmaid to pay me $60 to cover dry cleaning expense. Buddy's mom and my mom picked out all the flowers, decorations, the menu, music, and the photographer. The groomsmen had their black tuxedos and their cummerbunds to match the dresses. My dad was giving me away, Matthew would hand his dad the ring to put on me, and Destiny would be our flower girl. After Destiny dropped the flowers, she would remain beside me during the wedding.

I did not know what type of wedding band Buddy got me, but I had gotten Buddy's band personally made. It had three rows of diamonds and our twins' ruby birthstone on both sides of the diamonds. I knew Buddy would be surprised and all emotional, but I felt he deserved the most beautiful ring there was. The only way it could have been that special was if I had it made for him.

It was our wedding day and we were ready. Buddy and I were standing before God, our children, and our parents. It was finally happening. I was marrying the love of my life and finally getting the man of my dreams. *Somebody please pinch me, but do not wake me up,* I was thinking to myself. I was crying, Buddy was crying, and our parents were crying. The twins looked like they wanted to cry, but they were kids and found it embarrassing to show too much emotion.

We finally said, "I do." We kissed and had been announced as Mr. and Mrs. Matthew Buddy Dorsey, II. Dr. Matthew Buddy Dorsey, II and Attorney Autumn French-Dorsey were finally husband and wife. Our twins were so excited. Buddy and I could not stop blushing. We blushed, we admired our children, and we showed much gratitude to our parents. My dad could not stop smiling at me. Our moms could not stop entertaining and hugging us. I knew we had made our parents so proud. Our parents wanted to treat us to an extravagant honeymoon, but Buddy and I just wanted to be married. Nothing else mattered. We promised each other we would take a honeymoon in the future.

We took so many pictures with the bridal party, with our children, alone, with our parents, and with the entire family. This was a day that would not be forgotten. The reception ended late. We insisted that all the guests who live a distance away stay between Buddy's parents' house and our house. Buddy's parents had a guest house with four bedroom and our new home had an in-law house. My mom and dad stayed in our in-law house, along with some of my brothers. My brother Adam and his girlfriend stayed in the house with us. We had enough room for more people, but they refused. Buddy and I insisted that our children stay home with us.

Buddy and I were so amazed and excited that we sat with our clothes on half the night. Buddy kept talking to my brother and his girlfriend. Our relationship was not based on sex, but on true love. Buddy walked and talked all night. When we finally settled in, we fell on the bed and quickly went to sleep.

The next morning, Buddy and I woke up laughing about our night. Buddy's phone was ringing.

"Good morning, Mom," answered Buddy. "Autumn, my mom wants everyone to come to their house for brunch." We all got dressed and went to Buddy parents' house. After brunch Buddy's mom insisted the twins stay with them for a few days to give Buddy and I some privacy. My mother-in-law asked Buddy to bring them enough clothes for the week and he said he would bring them back a little later." We could not stop talking about our new life, reflecting and making plans for our future. We had matured from our college days. Maturity is important in this life.

The Flower is Blooming

*O*ur twins transferred to the Gastonia, North Carolina school district. It had been six months. The children were comfortable in their new school. I was comfortable commuting back and forth to the office twice a week. Working from home gave me the opportunity to take care of my family. Buddy had converted his den into a beautiful, spacious home office with all the necessary office equipment. My secretary emailed, faxed and overnighted everything needed. My dad was satisfied with the work arrangement. My brother Adam was heading the new office in Weaverville. I was representing clients from both offices. Our firm was doing well, as was Buddy and his parents' medical practice.

Our twins would be 12 years old soon. They were growing up quickly. I was now a member at Buddy's church. My granddad was sad to see me go, but he agreed with my decision. I must admit, I missed my friends, and especially my grandparents. But I know it was the right thing to do. Buddy and I had a date night and we scheduled a family night. We both recognized the importance of having quality time with your loved ones. Every now and then we would seek to have a movie night, sometimes with our twins and sometimes we watched movies alone. Buddy insisted on having a housekeeper, because he did not want me to overdo it. Also, I did not want me to neglect myself. So I agreed with his decision.

Life was moving fast. We were coming up on one year of marriage. I wanted to plan something nice, but Buddy asked me to arrange a quiet dinner for two. I wanted to please my husband, so I did as Buddy asked. My plans were to cook, but I had been a feeling extra tired lately. Buddy asked me to come to his office to make sure I did not have any vitamin deficiencies. Due to a conflict of interest, I had to see Buddy's associate, Dr. Patrick Newkirk. Dr. Patrick took blood and urine samples and gave me a thorough routine examination. He promised to contact me if the test revealed anything out of the ordinary. For now, he advised me to get plenty of rest, drink plenty of fluids, and eat healthy. "No takeout for now," said Dr. Patrick.

Four days later Dr. Patrick had the nurse call to ask me to come in and meet with him. I was concerned because that meant something had been found. The only time a doctor ever called a patient to come back in for a follow-up exam was because there was some form of medical condition that had to be discussed. What could be wrong? I exercised three days a week and drank plenty of water. There was no history of cancer, high blood pressure, diabetes, or heart disease in my family that I was aware of. We were always health conscious people. I decided not to alarm Buddy. Buddy never mentioned anything, and I decided to not say anything for now. Buddy not knowing could be a good sign. I did not know if Dr. Patrick would have shared anything with Buddy or if he could legally share my medical information. The Health Insurance Portability and Accountability Act of 1996 (HIPAA) had strict guidelines in place to protect patients. I struggled to act normal and not show any concern.

As I was opening the door to the doctor's office, Buddy was standing at the receptionist's desk. He seemed very surprised to see me. "Why are you back here?" he asked, "I don't recall you telling me you had an appointment."

"Dr. Patrick asked me to come back in today. Buddy looked worried. He said, "We will talk after you meet with Dr. Patrick." The nurse called my name.

"Yes, here I am," I responded. I walked to the examination room the nurse directed me to. I sat there waiting patiently for Dr. Patrick. When he entered the room, he greeted me.

"Hi, Mrs. Dorsey, how are you?"

"I need you to tell me, doc," I replied. I was nervous and shaking while Dr. Patrick reviewed my medical records. Then the moment of truth came.

"Ms. Dorsey, we got your test results back and the test shows you are pregnant," said Dr. Patrick. My mouth was wide open and I was shocked. Buddy and I did not plan on another child. I began to worry about what Buddy was going to say and how was he going to react.

Dr. Patrick had the nurse make me an appointment to see a gynecologist. I began to think I was so busy that I ignored that fact I did not have a menstrual in a few months. I asked Dr. Patrick not to tell Buddy or let him find out. I wanted to be the one to speak to him first.

"I will not tell him," said Dr. Patrick.

"Thank you, Dr. Patrick," I said. I asked the nurse, "Where is Dr. Buddy?"

"He is with a patient in one of the examination rooms. Would you like for me to tell him you want to see him?" she asked. I do not think I even responded. I rushed out of the office. I was not prepared to tell Buddy, answer any questions, or see his reaction.

When Buddy arrived home, I pretended to be asleep. It was Friday and I asked my mom to come get the twins for the weekend. She was always pleased to know they were coming to her house. Since we lived in Gastonia, she did not see them as often as she would like. I felt Buddy sit down on the bed, but he was always concerned about me, so he did not attempt to wake me up. He walked into the family room and I heard the television come on. Then I heard the microwave door open and shut. I was accustomed to leaving Buddy's food in the microwave. Sometimes he had to stay late at work or do something special at the church. I was so glad I texted him a message that the twins were staying at my mom's. That was the only reason he would have awakened me. Those children were his life. He was a great father. I wondered if he was ready to be a new dad again. I knew it would be a new experience for him because he did not find out about the twins until they were six years of age.

The next morning, I was awaked by the smell of breakfast. I took my shower, put on my jeans and T-shirt, did my hair, and put on a light coat of make-up. As I was exiting our bedroom, Buddy asked, "Are you hungry?"

I said, "Yes, thank you for doing this." Buddy continued to stare at me, and I refused to give him eye contact.

Finally, Buddy said, "Autumn, please talk to me. What did the doctor say? Please do not keep anything from me."

I looked up and our eyes met. I said, "Buddy, I am pregnant."

"You are pregnant?" Buddy leapt up from his chair and began to rejoice. Then Buddy made his way over to me and passionately kissed me. After several minutes of leaping and yelling, Buddy sat down and asked, "Do you want this baby?"

"Buddy, I would have ten children if it would make you happy. This was unplanned and I thought you would be upset."

Buddy grabbed my hand and said, "Baby, I love you. A baby with you can never be a mistake. Anything we produce, is produced out of love." I cried with relief and Buddy embraced me. "Autumn, I will always love and support you. Please do not ever keep anything from me. I do not care how you think I will react."

"Buddy, I will never do that again."

I was so happy about Buddy's reaction to the news of us having a new baby. He waited on me the entire weekend. Between him and the housekeeper, I could not do anything. He continued to ask me, "How do you feel?" I assured him I was great. I did not have morning sickness like with the twins. As Buddy and I were holding each other, Buddy and I made a pact to go to every doctor's appointment together. I had married a good man. No man is perfect, but he loved God and he loved me. My life had come to the blooming stage and now my family and I were blossoming.

The Season is Expanding

O ur parents were ecstatic to learn they were going to be grandparents again. Buddy was so happy to be a dad again, and the
twins were deciding how they would act as a big brother and sister
to our addition to the family. Of course, my dad had the nerve to say,
"Suppose you have twins again?" I was not trying to hear that at all.
I would just laugh and would not respond. My mom knew that I did
not like it, but she would not say anything in front of me. She would
just give my dad a strange look. When Buddy's parents found out
about the baby, they drove directly to our house. I did not know who
was happier, Buddy or his parents.

The twins were going through this phase where one wanted to
overpower the other. They argued every other day. "I am the oldest,
Destiny!" Matthew would yell.

"No, you're not!" Destiny would respond. Then Buddy and I
would here, "Mom, tell Matthew who is the oldest."

"Matthew, Destiny came into this world a few minutes before
you. The two of you are twins, born on the same day, and your parents love you both very much," I would say. Buddy would just laugh.
In the beginning of the twins' new phase, Buddy would look so sad.
I felt a lot of guilt because I felt like I robbed him of sharing his children's birth and early childhood.

Buddy and I went to all the gynecologist appointments
together. We were keeping our monthly appointments. I was now six

months pregnant and the doctor wanted to do an ultrasound. Buddy and I both agreed that we did not want to know the sex of the baby. We wanted to be surprised.

I was now 32 years of age and Buddy was 34. During dinner after our doctor's appointment I asked Buddy if we could have a private conversation. I wanted to ask him an important question. "How many children are we having?"

Buddy smiled. "Baby, how many children do you want to have? You want 10 or 15?" I wanted to slap Buddy.

"No, I would like to have one more."

Buddy said, "That is fine with me. Can we wait a few years after our new baby?"

"Of course."

The next day I was working from home. Buddy and Destiny came home early. Destiny ran upstairs to her room. I asked, "What is wrong?"

Buddy said, "Destiny's menstrual has started. She was so scared, she kept calling my phone. I picked her up from school early." Buddy looked worried. I went to Destiny's room and talked to her about caring for herself and good hygiene, especially around that time of the month.

"Can I lay down for a nap?" asked Destiny.

"Yes, daughter," I replied.

When Destiny closed the door and I was heading back downstairs, Buddy proclaimed, "Our baby is finally growing into a woman." I just smiled. Destiny was built like a woman and wore a D cup. I guess Buddy could not see that Destiny had been growing into a woman for the last year. Then again, that really did not matter, at

32 years of age my dad still saw me as his baby girl. Matthew rushed in the door from school.

"What is wrong, Dad? Is Destiny okay?" he asked. We assured him that she was fine, and that he did not have to worry. As much as they argued, they really loved each other. That reminded me of the way I would argue with my brothers, especially Adam.

I was now seven months pregnant. I was not as big as I was with the twins. My feet were not as swollen, and I carried this baby in a more attractive way. That was a relief because I did not want another set of twins. It was the weekend that our parents decided to throw us a baby shower. Since, Buddy and I did not know the sex of the baby, our moms had the shower decorated in blue, pink, and silver. This was a good opportunity to see a lot of our friends and family. Buddy and I had been busy with our family, church, and our careers. This first year we really bonded, and the family time was needed. Our shower was packed. Buddy watched my every move. He was so attentive. I felt so robbed because I did not have this type of attention from him with the twins even though I know it was my choice.

We had received a lot of gifts. There were all sorts of gifts. We received gift cards, cash, diapers, and sleepers. Buddy and I had finally decided to sell my property and expand our current property. We had already built a master bedroom on the first floor and now we were going to add a room for the baby. The twins would remain upstairs on the second floor of the house. In addition to a new baby and renovating our home, Buddy was about to become the pastor of our local church. His pastor was retiring due to his health. Buddy and I would continue to serve and make sure we had enough time for our family.

Wow! I was eight months pregnant and I could not wait for my baby to be delivered. *Wait!* The bed was wet. "Buddy, Buddy, please get up," I nervously asked.

"What is wrong, baby?" asked Buddy.

"My water broke, and the bed is wet," I told him. He looked at his cell phone and it was 3:00 AM. He immediately called his parents and his sister came to our house right away. Buddy and I went to the hospital and Buddy called my doctor to meet us there. It was the same drill as when I had the twins. Dr. Herman met us at the door and told us he would have to induce my labor because my water had broken. He said, "Dr. Dorsey, if you want to go home you can. We will take very good care of your wife. As you know it could be several hours before she is ready to go into labor."

Buddy said, "I appreciate it, but I am staying right here with my wife."

I asked Buddy, "Do you mind if I go to sleep?" I felt if I went to sleep the pain would be gone by the time I woke up. I could not take the pain of giving birth. It hurt so bad with the twins.

Buddy said, "Of course baby. Go to sleep. I am not leaving your side. I will be right here in this chair." I was awakened a couple of times by Buddy's phone ringing. My family kept calling to check on me and see if the baby was born.

I was finally awakened by sharp pains around 10:00 AM. I took a quick glance at the clock on the wall. "Buddy, Buddy," I cried.

"Yes, baby, I am right here with you," said Buddy as he was pushing the button for the nurse. "Buddy, please give me something for the pain," I pleaded.

"Buddy said, "Baby I can't.

In walked Dr. Herman and Buddy stepped back because they had to see if I had dilated enough centimeters to give birth. Herman checked me and said, "Autumn, it is time to deliver your baby." It seemed like years had passed.

"Push, push!" yelled Dr. Herman and Buddy.

The baby was here. "It is a boy," said Buddy. We both were crying tears of joy. My life's season was in full bloom.

Chillier Temperatures Have an Impact

*O*was awakened by a bad dream. I could not even remember what the dream was about. It was disturbing. I did not even want to go back to sleep, but it was Friday and I had two days to sleep late. The house was just too quiet. I reached for my cellphone to see what time it was. It was still early. It was 8:15 PM. I looked at my call log and saw that I had three missed calls from a former client of mine, Darla. It appeared she had left me a message. I would call her once I found out where in the house my family were.

I came out of our bedroom and Buddy was nowhere in the house. I could hear Matthew practicing in his room. There was no sound coming from Destiny's room, and I saw the light on in Braxton's room. "Buddy, Matthew, Destiny, Braxton, are you here?" I yelled out. Destiny came to the door of her room. "Daughter, is where is everyone at?" I asked.

Destiny said, "Matthew and Braxton are in their rooms. Dad is not here." She then went right back in her room like I was disturbing her. I glanced at my cell phone for a second time, but there were no calls or texts from Buddy to say he would be home late. This was so unlike him. Suddenly, Matthew exited his room.

"Hi, Mom," He said.

"Hi, son, have you heard from your dad?" I asked.

"No, I tried to call him a few times and his phone went straight to voicemail." I dialed Buddy's cell phone. Just as Matthew had said, the voicemail came on immediately. I left a message saying, "Buddy, this is Autumn calling to make sure you are okay. Please call me or text me and let me now you are fine, babe." I was beginning to worry. Buddy would always call or text us if he was coming home past 6:00 PM. He knew I would wait up for him or have his dinner on the table. This was unusual. I began to pray for God to protect him and let him be safe.

I had to stay positive and keep the faith. It could have been an emergency. Since Buddy became the pastor of the church, he had a lot more responsibility, and sadly to say, we were not spending as much time together as we had in the past. Our relationship was a far cry from what it was in college, and from the beginning of our marriage, seven years ago. However, we made every effort to keep the spark in our marriage. A lot was changing and about to change. The twins were about to go to college and Braxton was now six years of age. Both Buddy and I had been well known around North Carolina due to our involvement in the church, and our professional reputations.

Let me call Darla to see what is so important that she had to call three times. "Attorney Dorsey, this is Darla. Please call me when you get the opportunity." That was the message that Darla left for me.

"Good evening, may I speak to Darla? This is Attorney Autumn Dorsey." I said to the woman on the opposite end of the phone. Darla and I had not talked for a while, so I was not sure if she answered the telephone or someone else.

"This is Darla. Thank you for calling me back, Attorney Dorsey. I was concerned and do not want to be the bearer of bad news. I work in a restaurant in Cherryville, and I just saw your husband here with another woman," said Darla. I was becoming annoyed because my husband's spiritual and professional career could cause him to meet up with anyone, anywhere. "The only reason I am calling is because they looked quite chummy, feeding each other from their plates, laughing and touching the entire night." By this time during the call, I was furious, first because Buddy never called or texted to say he was late. No matter what, I could not let Darla sense that or say something to her I might regret later.

Darla replied. "They left about ten minutes ago."

Now my worry had turned to suspicion. I continued to ask myself, *why would Buddy travel 25 minutes outside of Gastonia to meet with a strange woman for dinner?* Each second that Buddy was not home I was becoming more and more furious. I thought there should be a good explanation as to why this all was happening. Darla's words played over and over in my head, and tons of questions began to surface that I needed answers to. It was 8:40 PM, and Buddy should be walking in the door any minute. I had every intention of remaining calm and finding out exactly what was going on with my husband and this woman. I called Buddy again at 9:15 PM. He was not home, and his phone continued to go to voicemail. I felt it was only fair that I texted him a strong message: "Pastor Dorsey, this is Autumn. What is going on? One of my former clients saw you in a restaurant in Cherryville with a strange woman. The two of you were feeding each other and having a good time. You left me here to worry and did not call your family to let us know that you would be coming home late."

It was getting later and later. Our children had never seen us argue or fight. I figured I better call my mother-in-law. "Hi, Mom," I said.

"Hi, Autumn, is everything okay?" my mom-in-law asked with concern.

"Yes, Mom, I want to send the kids over to your house. I will get Matthew to drive them over there for the night. Is that okay?" I asked.

"Autumn, what is going on with you and Buddy?" my mom-in-law asked with deep concern.

"Mom, it is not anything bad. Buddy and I have a situation. It is better that the children are not here," I said with gratitude.

Send them over, Autumn," said my mother-in-law.

"Matthew, Destiny, and Braxton, please pack a bag. You all are staying at your grandmother's house," I yelled. Matthew and Destiny ran to the door. Simultaneously, the twins asked, "Why, Mom? What is going on? Where is Dad?"

"Matthew, I need you to drive all of you over to your grandmother's house," I replied in a strong manner.

Matthew ran down the steps to me and asked, "Mom, what is wrong?"

"Nothing, son. I need you to do this for me. Your dad and I must talk in private. Please do this for me, son," I pleaded.

"Okay, Mom, we will go over there, but I will keep calling Dad to see what is going on," said Matthew.

The children had left, and it was 9:35 PM. Buddy still had not arrived at home. Now I am thinking about packing me a bag and running to my mom in Black Mountain. The only thing that was stopping me was our children. I owed it to them to try to salvage our family. I called Buddy's telephone number again. This time his phone was ringing, therefore, I knew he got my text. Was he hesitating to come home because he was ashamed or was he guilty?

I heard a car approaching our home. I said to myself, *Matthew better not have dropped off his sister and brother and turned to come back home.* I jumped up and looked out the window. I could tell it was Buddy's car approaching. I ran back to the chair to sit down. It seemed as if Buddy was taking hours to come inside of the house and face me. I heard Buddy's key turning. When Buddy crossed the threshold, I could see the nervousness in his face. I believe Buddy saw the anger in my eyes.

"Autumn, can we talk?" asked Buddy. "Are the kids here?"

"Matthew drove them to your mom's house," I replied. "I called your mom to ask if they could stay there tonight, so we could talk," I told Buddy. Buddy sat down beside me. My eyes were filled with tears that masked my anger and disappointment.

Buddy took a deep breath before speaking, "Autumn, I apologize for not being open and honest. I never told you the details of my divorce with Summer. I agreed to pay spousal support for five years or until she got married. She had been repeatedly calling the office and I would not return her call. Today she showed up without my knowledge. When I was getting in my car to come home, she was waiting for me in the parking lot. She seemed quite desperate, and I was not sure what she wanted or what was behind all the phone calls. When I saw her, my thoughts were to settle this once and for all, get her away from my office, and to take care of this matter before you found out. I took her to dinner. All I could think about was getting her to leave me alone. My mind was preoccupied, and I did not want her to find out where we live by following me home. I followed her to Cherryville, where she said she was staying," explained Buddy.

"What about you the two of you feeding each other and rubbing each other's arms?" I asked.

"I was wrong. She was flirting and I flirted back with her, which is wrong since I am married to you. I tried to find a thousand ways to tell you that I had to pay Summer money. I knew we hurt you and I did not want to cause you any more pain," cried Buddy.

"You did! Are you still paying her? What is the arrangement the two of you came up with, Buddy?" I asked in a serious manner. By this time, I was crying silently. Buddy saw the tears but could not hear my internal screams.

"Autumn, I simply told her that I could not help her any longer. Apparently, she lost her job and did not save any of the money I had given her over the years," said Buddy. "Basically, she wanted my financial help and needed more money that I dare not give to her," said Buddy.

"I trusted you. Why couldn't you trust me and tell me what was going on?" I asked Buddy. Buddy continued to stare, waiting for me to continue my thoughts on the subject. I stood up and walked to our bedroom.

"Autumn, please do not walk away from me. Come on, baby, please. Let's talk," asked Buddy. I heard Buddy gasp and it sounded like whimpering. We were both hurting, and Buddy had destroyed my trust in him again.

Matthew was calling our phones repeatedly during the entire conversation. I could not bring myself to talk to him, because I did not want my son to hear the pain in my voice. I heard Buddy answer his phone. "Hi, son." I could not hear what Matthew was saying, but Buddy kept replying, "Son, everything is okay. I need all of you to stay at your grandmother's house for the weekend. I have some making up to do with your mom. Everything will be okay, son. We are family. Families have to overcome things in this life, but we will be okay." I was emotional, but I dared not cried out loudly. I cried while I prayed. I did not know how to react. I knew I could not push my husband away, but I could not experience the heartache of his betrayal again. When I heard Buddy coming toward the bedroom, I pretended to be asleep. I felt Buddy staring at me, but I refused to acknowledge him. I could not stay here. Tomorrow I would get up and go to have a me day. That was my plan and I was going to stick with it.

I was awakened by a beautiful aroma. I got in the shower and got dressed to go out alone. "Good morning," Buddy said.

"Good morning, Buddy," I replied.

Buddy asked, "Are you hungry? I made you this delicious breakfast." I had my pocketbook on my arm, and I was dressed to go out. "Are you going somewhere?" asked Buddy.

"Yes, I am going to do some things," I replied while walking swiftly to the door. Buddy hurried behind me and grabbed my arm.

"Autumn, please don't leave. Can we spend the day together?" he asked.

Then it fell out of my mouth. "I am hurt, Buddy. Why did you feel you had to hide something like this from me? It affected both of us. What is the most hurtful is that you had to have a private account set up because I would have noticed large sums of money being deducted on a monthly basis." Buddy dropped his head. I did not realize what I was saying, but at that moment I knew how all those payments were hidden from me. This was an even deeper betrayal. What else could my husband be hiding? Then I asked the most important question. "Is she worth jeopardizing your family and destroying our marriage?"

I couldn't complete the sentence without Buddy yelling, "No, not at all! Baby there is nothing more important to me than God, you, and our children. I will make this up to you. What do you want me to do to make this right?"

I quickly responded, "I want you to not hide anything from me again, and I want you to cease from contacting Summer. Also, I need you to treat me as a partner. Before you make those types of decisions that affects us, I need you to discuss that with me." Buddy agreed. He kissed me softly. We spent every moment together on that Saturday and I knew our love was strong. Throughout the day we found ourselves holding each other like we just could not let go.

Even in chillier times our love continued to grow.

The Seeds are Sprouting

*I*t was Matthew and Destiny's prom day. Matthew was taking Buddy's colleague's daughter, Sadie, to the prom. Destiny was going with her boyfriend, who Buddy did not care for. Buddy was so nervous. The twins wanted to drive individually to the prom. Buddy insisted they go in one limo and he was not taking "no" for an answer. I must admit, Buddy was the authoritative one in our family. Buddy gave them an option: either they take one limo, or he would personally drive them. They took the limo. Matthew would try to get me alone and persuade me to talk to his dad. I assured Matthew there was no way I was going against his dad's decision. After all, they were going to the same location at the same time.

The twins were going to college. Destiny was going to live in the dorm and Matthew was going to commute from home. Matthew was majoring in music and Destiny was majoring in biology. Destiny was following in her dad's career path to become a doctor. Matthew was musically gifted. He could play almost any instrument made and boy, he could sing. I know he got that from my brothers. In fact, Matthew was his dad's minister of music. He traveled everywhere with his dad when it came to church fellowship and business.

The prom night was not good for Buddy. When the clock got to 12:15 AM, he paced the floor and continued to look out the window. I saw he picked up his phone several times and was dialing. I dared not ask if he was calling Matthew or Destiny. I just smiled out of gratitude. My children had the pleasure of enjoying the life experience of having a father and mother who care. Finally, I could not take it anymore. "Babe, come lay down," I insisted.

Buddy answered in a rough manner, "I will, Autumn." I knew it was just his concern for his children. I could not take the tone personal. Buddy jumped up and headed towards the living room. "It must be Matthew and Destiny," I said to myself. I glanced at my cellphone and it was 1:15 AM. I was proud of them. Their dad rented the limo and the driver until 2:00 AM. Buddy hurried to the bedroom and pretended he was not worrying or pacing. He sat by the door waiting to hear something. All I could do was quietly laugh.

I was awakened again by the smell of breakfast. Buddy did not cook on a regular basis. I was starting to see a pattern here. After all these years, I had finally figured it out. Buddy would convert to Chef Buddy when he wanted to gather, right a wrong, or prepare you to answer his questions. A friend of mine called it "checking your temperature." Buddy would monitor your actions, responses, and behavior. He always seemed to launch the questions or start the conversation at the right time.

"Breakfast is ready," yelled Buddy from the dining room. It was during the days of Chef Buddy's full course breakfast I was so grateful for our housekeeper Dorothy. Buddy would create such a mess. Dorothy was used to Buddy's methods of cooking. You would see Buddy leave the kitchen and Dorothy go in. Buddy was not accustomed to washing the dishes or loading the dishwasher as he was cooking. Everything would be left in the same place. Dorothy and I would laugh as they would appear to be playing revolving doors. When I cooked, I would wash the dishes and load the dishwasher. Not Buddy. The sink would be stacked, and the counters would be a mess.

Everyone exited their rooms when they heard that breakfast was finished. I prayed the twins would be ready for Daddy's Q & A. Buddy blessed the food and we all began to eat. Buddy took a deep breath. "So how was the prom?" he asked. He did not care who answered. Buddy just wanted details. "Did Sadie have a good time, Matthew?" Matthew always reminded me of my dad. You give him the opportunity and he would tell it all. Matthew covered the details of his evening, but Destiny remained silent. She was more like her dad than he cared to acknowledge. Buddy continued to glance at Sadie. Sadie remained silent and did not stop eating. Buddy was antsy. Finally, he asked, "Sadie, did you have a good time?"

Sadie simply said, "Yes." That was not enough for her dad. He took another deep breath. "What did you do at the prom with your boyfriend?" asked Buddy. Matthew and I wanted to run and laugh, but we knew we better not.

"We had a great time. I will miss my high school friends, but I am looking forward to starting college," replied Sadie.

Buddy looked at me, and I quickly noted, "Your dad and I are glad to hear both of you had a wonderful time. That is all we wanted."

I know Buddy had a lot more questions. I was just glad he did not ask them.

Our family had a busy summer scheduled before Destiny went off to college. Adam was marrying his long-time girlfriend, Ashley. My brother, Robert, was about to become a father. My dad kept insisting he marry Jenna. My parents were just as supportive to Robert and Jenna as they were to me. Robert had recently graduated from medical school and was working in the local hospital in Asheville, North Carolina. The French clan never strayed too far from home. Even my dad stayed closed to his parents. My mom's parents passed away when she was young. I barely remembered them. My mom was their only biological daughter, but they had adopted three daughters before my mom. My mom always said that she was grateful for her older sister. Her mom and dad were under the impression they could not have any children. They called my mom a miracle. My mom was my miracle and my blessing. I would do anything for her. Sometimes I would call my mom just so I could hear her say, "Daughter."

"Babe, I want to purchase Destiny a new car," said Buddy. Matthew already had a new car because he got paid to play music at a lot of different venues. We knew our daughter was going to college two and a half hours away at Duke University. We were happy that her and Sadie were going to be roommates.

"That is a great idea, baby," I said to Buddy. Buddy took Destiny to the car dealer alone. I knew he needed that time with his daughter. Then Buddy came up with this fantastic idea of following Destiny to college. I had agreed because I could see he was going through something with her leaving home for school. Buddy was not talkative at all. I broke the ice when I said, "Baby, she will be fine. Destiny is your daughter. She has your drive, personality, and character."

Buddy smiled and said, "I know. She is not our baby anymore."

I said, "She will always be our baby." I believe I got a glimpse into how my dad felt when I moved away from home to go to college. There is something about a man's bond with his daughter. I am confident Sadie and Destiny will be fine. The seeds planted by Buddy and I were sprouting.

Growth Requires Dirt

CHAPTER 13

"How did you sleep?" asked Buddy.

"I slept well," I replied. Buddy and I both broke out in a laugh. Buddy leaned over to kiss me.

"I will see you at church. I want to go pray before service."

"Okay," I replied. Matthew and Braxton had stayed at my parents' house for the weekend. They would meet us at the church this morning. Buddy and I woke up so excited. Our family was going through a lot of transitions with our twins stepping into adulthood and Buddy's church leadership creating a lot of growth and advancement for the ministry. The overseer and the congregation were well pleased. I believe God was pleased as well. Buddy had decided to spend more time working in the church and decrease his days at the medical practice. I believe he was holding on until Destiny could take over. I recognized that Buddy had to service from 300 to over 1,500 people in five years. Each Sunday it appeared more people were joining the congregation. Buddy continued to ordain deacons to help in the ministry and he ordained additional ministers.

There were times I wanted to leave, but I always remembered my mom telling me, "No matter what happens, a woman does not leave her home or abandon her family under any circumstances." There were many occasions on which I chose humility and remained kind to my husband. It caused me to be a better person and it caused my husband to be a better man.

When I arrived at the church service was just getting started. Buddy was not sitting on the pulpit. I assumed he was still in the back preparing to deliver the morning message. Buddy always insisted I sit on the pulpit because I was an ordained minister. I just felt more comfortable sitting in the pews with everyone else. While I was sitting the usher rushed over to get my attention and said, "Pastor Dorsey needs to see you right away."

I began praying, "Please do not let anything be wrong with Destiny or any other member of our family." Matthew was sitting at the organ and Braxton was on the drums, so I knew they were fine. I knocked on Buddy's office door.

"Come in," he yelled. I walked in and Buddy rose from his chair. "Babe, I need you to pray for the service today," he said. When I looked at the printed program, I recognized the name of the person that was supposed to pray, and she was there in the congregation.

"Pastor, is everything ok," I asked. When at church. I recognized who he was.

"Yes, for now. We will talk later," said Buddy. I did not want to pressure him knowing he had to preach the morning message, so, I was obedient. I prayed for the congregation and for the pastor to be used by God like never before. I could always tell when it was God and when it was me. The sounds of praise were silenced and when I said "Amen" I could hear just how loud the congregation was. I was always grateful and honored to be used by God. I felt something had been changed. I just did not know what it was.

At the end of service, Buddy would always stand at the front of the church to greet everyone. I would stand where I was and talk to people at well, and I made sure to embrace my in-laws, who were always good to me. My mom and my mother-in-law talked on the phone every day. They had become besties. I saw the strange look on Buddy's mom's face and his dad didn't look too thrilled as Buddy was talking to a strange woman. As an attorney, I had trained myself to read facial expressions and body language. Now I was thinking, *what is going on?*

I turned around and noticed Buddy was looking at me. He was standing there talking to a woman I did not recognize. He began to signal for me to come where he was. I walked up to Buddy, and he immediately kissed me and grabbed me around my waist. "Baby, I would like for you to meet my ex-wife, Summer. Summer, this is the love of my life, Autumn," said Buddy. I could not pretend that I was not shocked to meet Summer. I thought I would never hear her name again. She was attractive and the two of us kind of favored. Even our eye color was similar.

"Nice to meet you, Summer," I said as I stuck my hand out to shake hers. "Baby, what are we doing? Are we going to going to dinner or one of our parents' houses?" I asked Buddy, letting Summer know I no longer considered her a threat. I felt her eyes examining every inch of me. I know she was asking herself, *what does she have that I don't?* If the question would have arose the answer would have been simple: Buddy, Matthew, Destiny, and Braxton. Buddy began to pour it on heavy. "We are going to dinner alone. I want you all to myself," said Buddy.

Summer quickly interrupted. "Nice to finally meet you, Autumn." I wanted to tell her she met me the night she called my phone, but there was no sense in being petty now.

"Nice to meet you too, Summer. Come worship with us again. Baby, I will meet you at your car," I said as I was walking away.

As I was walking out, I heard, "Mom." I know my children's voices. I turned around as Braxton was rushing toward me.

"Yes, son," I replied.

Braxton said, "Matthew and I are going over to our grandmother's house to eat." They loved her cooking. So did I.

"Okay, son, let your dad know," I replied. Before I got to the car Buddy was right behind me. I saw the puzzled look on his face. To lighten everything I asked, "Did Braxton tell you they were going to your mom's house to eat? Do you want to go there?"

Buddy said, "That is up to you." I sat down in Buddy's car for a private conversation. I had driven my own car today. Buddy rushed to say, "Baby, I apologize that my past mistakes keep surfacing at the wrong times. I did not invite her, and I told her she would not embarrass me, my wife, or my children. I simply let her know if I even thought about helping her. That ship has sailed." I looked at Buddy and took notice to how upset he was. I wanted to say, "What do you mean you thought about helping her?"

Instead I took the humble road and said, "Buddy, everyone needs God. She can never embarrass us. I feel kind of sorry for her. She doesn't even recognize that her actions are disrespectful." Buddy just shook his head in agreement with what I was saying. "As far as your past, we are who we are due to our pasts. I stand with you, and I will never let anyone come between us."

Buddy smiled and said, "That is why I love you so much." I guess I just needed the assurance that Buddy loved me and that he was standing with me. I did not want him to disrespect Summer, although Summer continued to disrespect me. You cannot grow without life's dirt.

Blooming is a Never-ending Process

*I*t was another quiet afternoon. Braxton was at school and Buddy was at work. I imagined Matthew was in the studio that his grandparents had built for him at the church. My phone rang for the first time all day. The caller ID read *Dad*. "Hi, Dad," I asked.

My dad replied, "Hi, baby girl." My dad called me baby girl and my mom called me daughter. Both were great terms of endearment. "I need to come over and talk to you and Buddy," my dad explained. "I talked with Buddy and he told me the two of you will have some time this weekend."

"Dad, why don't we drive over to your house this weekend? I do not get home much," I shared.

My dad quickly responded, "Of course. I will have a late lunch prepared."

"Okay, love you, Dad. We will see you this weekend." We both hung up with the words that have kept our family together like glue: "I love you." Of course, I was the one who always overthought everything, so I wanted to have things figured out before the lunch. *This must be important*, I thought to myself. *Knowing my dad, it is something major he wants to discuss.*

Buddy came home. I was glad because I wanted to question him like he questions everyone else. "Did you talk to my dad?" I asked.

Buddy said, "Yes."

"What is so important," I asked Buddy.

"I don't know but is sounded serious to me. I thought he was calling about the men's day events both of our churches are having," said Buddy.

"I know my dad. It is something. Brace yourself," I said.

"Well, we will definitely find out in a few days," yelled Buddy from the kitchen.

It was Saturday morning. Buddy and I did an hour workout in our workout room. Immediately following, we got dressed. "Are you ready," asked Buddy. I just shrugged my shoulders. I told Buddy to brace himself. We grabbed a few pieces of food and hurried out the door. When we arrived, my dad and mom were sitting on the porch with the table set for six. Buddy and I just looked at each other. *What is up my dad's sleeve?* I thought to myself. As always, my mom was quietly at work making sure everyone was be happy. My mom was a great cook. My brothers and I insisted my mom hire a cook, which she refused. She finally did get a housekeeper after I left. I guess I was the maid. My mom and I were the only two I knew who had a housekeeper and still helped with their chores. The French clan may have lived and looked like divas, but we were servants at heart.

My dad asked Buddy to pray over the food. While we were preparing our plates, Adam and Ashley were pulling up to my parents' home. My dad yelled, "Please hurry so I can share this good news I received." There were still two plates remaining for Matthew and Braxton. All the people in attendance led me to believe it had something to do with my family and the law firm. I kept looking at my mom and all she would do is smile. My dad began the conversation. "I got a call from the Gaston District Court. They have me for a reference." Now my mind was going a thousand miles a minute, because my brother and Ashley lived in Buncombe County and Ashley was a district court judge there. The words were not forming fast enough out of my dad's mouth. That left room for wild speculation. At this point I refused to look at Buddy, because I was too busy bracing myself. We had no idea what was coming next. "Baby girl, you've been nominated to be district court judge in Gaston County. They were calling me for a reference," said my dad.

"I never asked to be nominated. How did they get my name?" I asked.

"One of our colleagues nominated you because they knew you lived in that county and two of their district judges is retiring in a month," my dad replied. I couldn't help looking at Buddy now. Our eyes met. I was speechless. I was not getting a good feeling from his facial expression. I was assuming Buddy was growing as concerned as I was. We knew that our lives would change. We were comfortable with me working from home three days a week and at the office two days a week.

"Dad, this will affect our lives and our family. We have gotten used to my work schedule," I anxiously noted.

My dad said, "No, you will not be able to stay home three days a week, but you deserve this, baby girl for all of your years of hard work."

My mom finally spoke. "You have the experience and I know you will make a difference for a lot of people." My heart and mind began to open when I heard my mom say *make a difference for a lot of people.* I kept looking at Buddy for some type of reaction. Buddy was just silent. I quickly intervened for Buddy, before his silence became as noticeable to my family as it was for me.

"Dad, Buddy and I will discuss it. Who do I call to let them know my decision?" I asked. My dad handed me a piece of paper with all the information on it.

"That is great, Mom. It is a great opportunity, right, Dad?" Matthew said.

Buddy as cheerfully as possible said, "Yes, it is a great opportunity."

On the way home, Buddy was not very talkative. He was always super supportive, and I knew whatever I decided he would support, yet I wanted him to share his true feelings.

When we arrived home Buddy quickly said, "I am going to take a nap." I believe that was his way of letting me know he was not prepared to talk about the situation. I knew a lot was going on with him. I had to just give him his space until he was ready. I knew for sure I could not accept or decline until Buddy and I had that conversation and reached an agreement.

It was getting late, but I could not sleep. The conversation with my dad had me restless, not to mention, Buddy's reaction. I decided to stay up and watch Christmas movies. Around 11:00 PM, Buddy came out the room, I guess to see where I was, and he walked over to me, leaned down, and kissed me. "Are you upset with me?" I asked Buddy.

"No, baby, I just do not want us to rush and make a decision. I have gotten used to you being here. I know you worked hard for this and I know you would be perfect for the job. I will never stand in your way. Whatever you decide to do, you know I will support you," said Buddy. He sat down and said, "Autumn, I am going to be honest with you. Our parents have always controlled our lives. I know we want to make them all happy, but at this point in our lives we have to do what is best for us."

"I understand," I said.

"I know I seemed mad, but it seems your dad already accepted the nomination. I get that his office was asked for a recommendation. You've worked there since passing the bar exam. I just feel he should have had them contact you and give them the nomination themselves." Was Buddy right? Was my dad overstepping boundaries again? Of course, he was. That is what my dad did all his life.

I looked Buddy in the eyes. "Babe, what do you want me to do? If you say this will affect our home, then I will turn it down. Personally, I feel I could help more people and make an impact in our county," I explained to Buddy.

Buddy looked and me and said, "Okay then."

"Buddy, please, what is really going on?" I asked. This was completely out of his character.

He replied, "What do you want me to say, Autumn? Your mind is already made up." Then he asked me the question that I needed to answer, "What do you want to do?"

I said without thinking, "I want to sit on the bench and represent God first, then this county, and present the good side of the law. If you are not in agreement, I will not accept it under any circumstances. Please do not feel you are holding me back. You have supported me from day one, Buddy. We both agree nothing is more important than our family."

Buddy kissed me and said, "Autumn, accept the nomination," and kissed me again. I had got the feeling Buddy just wanted to make sure his feelings counted, and perhaps he needed the assurance that I would always put our family first.

Two days later, I called the President Judge of Gaston Cunty and left a message with his secretary that I accept the nomination for district court judge. I had two weeks to report to work. They had a swearing in ceremony and our entire family attended. A few of my colleagues attended. Buddy and I noticed one judge that continued to stare at me and whenever Buddy walked away, he would approach me. His name was Peter Reynolds. I did see a ring on his finger, and it was just odd. When Buddy would come back to where I was standing, Judge Reynolds would walk away. Neither Buddy nor I said anything, but I can tell Buddy felt the weirdness like I did.

I learned my case load would be a far cry from the three to four cases I would accept as an attorney. In order to provide the best possible outcome, I would have to go through every case with a fine-tooth comb. I shared with Buddy and our children that I would have some late nights, but I promised to keep them at a minimum. Everyone was okay, and most importantly, they were super proud of me.

Here's where things got weird. It was required that I install a state-of-the-art security system. During certain cases I was told I may have security at my door. If I received any type of threats the county would provide security immediately. Buddy asked the sheriff, "Do we need bodyguards?" The sheriff answered that sometimes we would. The whole thing made Buddy nervous. He was super protective of me and our children. He called contractors to brick off our property and install an electric gate. The security system would notify us before someone even turned in our driveway. We could see the car approaching and who was driving before they even got to the front of our door. I told him that if we needed it, I would not stand in the way of getting it done. I asked if we could just see what happened with all of this.

I arrived at Gaston County Courthouse. It was a huge white building. My office and courtroom were on the fourth floor. I would be handling criminal cases. I still could not believe I was a district judge. With my hands shaking, I greeted Samantha, my law clerk and Pamela, my secretary. They both led me to my office and assisted me with my schedule. There were about 20 cases a day that would come before me. Also, I had time scheduled in case there were trials instead of plea agreements. Pamela and Samantha were very helpful to me. They were going to lunch and that gave me time to call my family. Before I got to dial on the phone, there was a knock was at the door.

"Come in," I yelled. It was Judge Peter Reynolds with flowers in his hand to officially welcome me. "God, this is getting weirder and weirder," I said to myself.

It appeared that I was getting home closer and closer to 7:00 PM. Time was passing by so fast. I was missing more and more of Buddy's calls, and there were tons of unreturned texts. In the beginning Buddy would greet me, but now it was Braxton who was greeting me at the door. Buddy seemed so distant. Our roles were reversing. Instead of me having food ready and putting a plate in the microwave for Buddy, Buddy was doing all that for me. In fact, with a mild attitude Buddy would say, "Your food is in the microwave." I was growing concerned. I was honored and grateful for the opportunity, yet I did not know how to resolve this. Then to top it all off, I started liking the attention of Judge Reynolds. It became too much, but I just viewed it as platonic. My phone would begin to ring at night and in the morning. The caller was always Judge Reynolds. Buddy looked suspicious, but he never would say anything to me.

Buddy and I barely talked or texted during the day and at night we slept with our backs to each other.

I could not take it anymore. I had gotten the opportunity to talk to Buddy. He was sitting in the family room watching television. I sat beside him and began to rub his hand and massage his back. Buddy did not say a word or even acknowledge me. I said, "Baby, can we talk?"

Buddy aggressively replied, "Nothing is wrong, Autumn. I am just not used to you being here. This is going to take getting used to." Then Buddy turned to me and passionately kissed me with a statement that gave me hope. "We will just have to adjust," said Buddy.

"Buddy, I will not settle or sacrifice our happiness. If this all becomes too much please just say the word," I said to Buddy.

Then the man I fell in love with surfaced. "Autumn, you have sacrificed so much for me. You always stood by me during times I did not even recognize you had my back. No matter what the situation is, I, as your husband, will stand by you," said Buddy. The tears came down my eyes. They were tears of joy. I was so happy to hear those words spoken by my man. The process may be hard and go through several stages of change, but your family priorities must stay the same.

Bloom Times

Our twins had graduated from college. Destiny is now in medical school and Matthew had recorded his group's second CD. Braxton was the lead on several of the songs. Matthew was becoming more and more in demand and Braxton was being trained by Matthew to head the choir in his absence. Churches all over the United States were booking Matthew to perform. Social media had really caused Matthew and Buddy both to be known in cities and states that they had never traveled to. Buddy's messages were live streamed every Sunday. Matthew and his dad traveled together a lot. Buddy tried to schedule a lot of out of town engagements for the weeks that I did not have to work. We never let Buddy travel alone. The church always accompanied him to churches in proximity.

Me being a district court judge put in high demand. We seemed to have a lot of events to attend. Buddy would often accompany me, but I could not impose on him. Buddy and I would go over our weekly schedules and we made every attempt to keep our schedules. The schedules always included our date night. I tried to make sure that nothing would interfere with this quality time. There were times Buddy had to cancel, but I refused to complain.

Judge Peter Reynolds seemed to be giving me additional attention, beyond the abundance of attention I had already been receiving. I was still fairly new. I didn't want to make waves, but this situation was getting quite uncomfortable. I couldn't call it sexual harassment because he never said or did anything inappropriate.

Samantha knocked on my door after Judge Peter Reynolds left my office. "Judge Dorsey, may I speak with you in private?"

"Sure, Samantha. Have a seat," I insisted. "Judge Dorsey, please do not take this in the wrong way. Please be careful with Judge Reynolds."

I had to ask, "What do you mean be careful?"

"Judge Reynolds has a reputation for being a womanizer. He goes after single, married, and widowed women," said Samantha. I laughed because I found it funny.

"Samantha, I am happily married," I replied.

It was becoming more and more apparent that Judge Reynolds was up to something. He seemed to be calling me more and more. Each time his excuse would be he need personal advice. The calls were becoming frivolous. Whenever he called, I would answer right in front of Buddy. I had nothing to hide. One day I answered the phone with my back to Buddy. "Hi, Judge Reynolds, Peter." Judge Reynolds called to tell me about a gathering they were having for one of our colleagues. I responded, "I will let you know. I have to talk to my husband." When I turned around Buddy had a look of anger on his face.

"What was that about," Buddy inquired. I explained to Buddy what the conversation was about. "So now he's Peter?" asked Buddy. I did not know how to respond to that question. "He is calling you more and more. All times of night. Is he calling when I am not here?" asked Buddy?

"Baby, what are you implying. Why are you saying that to me?" I asked Buddy.

"Autumn, come on. You trying to tell me you don't recognize the unusual amount of attention he gives you at every event?" said Buddy. "Every time we attend an event together, he does not talk to you unless I walk away," Buddy continued. Buddy was so right, but I did not want to create any more alarm for Buddy. "Baby, please be careful and pay attention."

I answered, "I will."

When I got to work, I asked Pamela to call Judge Reynolds' chamber and ask him if I could speak with him. My secretary called me on the interoffice line before going to lunch and said, "Judge Reynolds is here to see you."

"Send him in," I replied. We shook hands and he held my hand a little too long for me, so I gently snatched my hand back. I had to keep it professional. "Judge Reynolds, thank you for coming so quickly," I said as I sat in the chair beside his. "I need to speak with you and ask for your assistance. I am asking you to please not call me at home anymore. My husband is growing quite concerned and going forward I will limit the events I attend. You may be aware that my husband is a medical doctor and a pastor of a church. We have a 12-year-old son who needs his mom and dad around." Judge Reynolds looked puzzled at that statement. In fact, Judge Reynolds looked surprised because I was assuming many women were over-taken by his attention, good looks, and charm.

I was certainly different because I was a woman who took her vows seriously, one who loved her husband, and a woman who was determined to keep her family together. Judge Reynolds said, "I truly apologize. That was not my intention. You are a beautiful woman."

"A beautiful married woman," I interjected. He promised to cease all contact and I was glad to hear it. I was a happily married woman. It really didn't matter, I just wanted Judge Reynolds to get the message to stay away from me. As we stood up, Judge Reynolds leaned over to embrace me. My office door opened and it was Buddy. I wanted to die right there.

"Is this what we are doing now?" asked Buddy. "Get your stuff and I will see you at home," demanded Buddy. Luckily, I had no cases before me after lunch. Judge Reynolds immediately left right behind Buddy. I had never seen Buddy so mad. I waited for Pamela to come back and told her I was leaving early. Buddy was waiting for me in the driveway. We went into the in-law's house. "What was that about?" asked Buddy. I began to explain to Buddy what had happened. He listened attentively. "Is this going to be a problem, Autumn?" asked Buddy.

"Baby, I promise you it will not be a problem. I was getting weirded out about him. If he approaches me again, I promise to report him for sexual harassment. I promise you, baby, it was innocent, and he never did anything like that in the past. I do not know if he felt compelled because I made it clear for him to stay away from me. I told him you were growing concerned with the attention he was paying to me. The last thing I told him is that I am a happily married woman." I hugged my husband so tightly and gently kissed him. "I only want you, baby, only you, "I said.

In was in that moment I realized that the very thing I vowed not to do I was doing. I was neglecting my family and I was losing my focus. I decided I would get home before my family and cook for them like I used to. I sat down with Samantha and Pamela and we found a way to make that happen at least three days a week.

On my first early day, I reached home and none of my family was there. I even yelled out their names and no one answered. By the time Buddy and Braxton walked in, it was apparent I was taking my role back. They heard me in the kitchen. Buddy ran to the kitchen and said, "Hey babe." He gave me a gentle soft kiss.

Braxton yelled, "Mom!" He held me so tightly. It was obvious that my family missed me as much as I missed them. "Go get ready for dinner," I said.

"I will go wash my hands and set the table," said Buddy.

Buddy blessed the food and we all sat down to eat like a family. We had not done this in months. It was a family tradition that had become foreign in our household. "Where is Matthew," I asked his dad. I had a place set for him, but Matthew was not at home. At that moment Matthew walked in with his girlfriend, Diamond.

"Hi, Mom," said Matthew as he headed toward me to embrace me with excitement.

"Hi, Judge Dorsey," said Diamond. Buddy immediately jumped up to get Diamond a place setting. We all sat down to the dinner table. I never realized how much I needed this and what I was missing. This was time I needed to have with my family. Destiny was the only one not there. We truly missed her. Buddy and the boys seemed so thrilled. It was at that moment that I decided I had to put my family at the top of my list. Seasons change, but people's transitions and family values do not. My life had come to full bloom.